A
SINGING BIRD
WILL COME

NAOMI IN HONG KONG

A SINGING BIRD WILL COME

NAOMI IN HONG KONG

内奥米

BY KARMEL SCHREYER

GREAT PLAINS FICTION

Great Plains Publications
420 – 70 Arthur Street
Winnipeg, MB R3B 1G7
www.greatplains.mb.ca

Great Plains Publications gratefully acknowledges the financial support provided
for its publishing program by the Government of Canada through the Book
Publishing Industry Development Program (BPIDP); the Canada Council for
the Arts; the Manitoba Department of Culture, Heritage and Citizenship; and
the Manitoba Arts Council.

Design & Typography by Gallant Design Ltd.
Printed in Canada by Kromar Printing

CANADIAN CATALOGUING IN PUBLICATION DATA

Main entry under title:
Schreyer, Karmel, 1964-
A singing bird will come
     ISBN 1-894283-30-9
I. Title.
PS8587.C487S56   2002   jC813'.54   C2002-910093-3
PZ7.S379352Si   2002

For Emi Celeste and Blaise Lily,
my muses and my inspiration—always.

—Mom

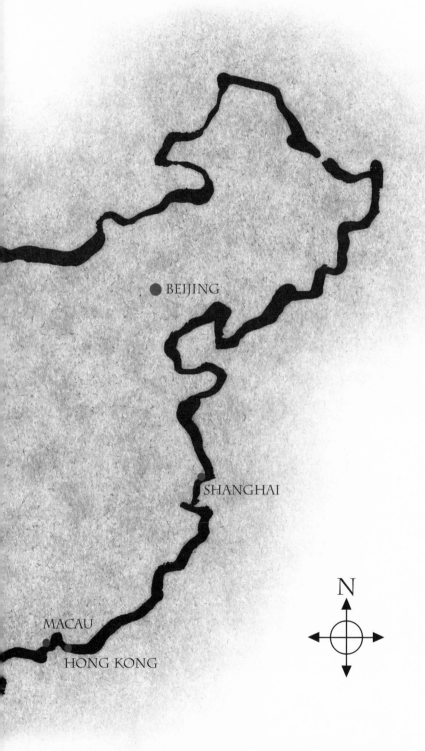

From wonder into wonder, existence opens.

—Chinese Proverb

"I've never seen hills as green as *that* before. And the *ocean*, Mom—it's awesome! So blue!" Naomi sat back in her chair, allowing her mother a peak through the window of the airplane.

Sara leaned across her daughter, craning her neck. "Those ships look just like little toys from way up here. Oh Naomi, I can see hundreds of skyscrapers on that island below us." She grinned at Naomi. "So *this* is Hong Kong!"

"Let me see," Naomi said. Excitement rang in her voice, and she gave her mother a little nudge with her head as she moved in for another look. "That's *got* to be downtown Hong Kong right there, Mom. So many buildings! Look at all the apartment blocks. We must be flying directly over Victoria Harbour." Naomi paused for a moment, then looked over at her mother, eyes wide. "Mom. It looks so—crowded."

Sara nodded. "You're right. Though we *were* warned, Naomi. Hong Kong is a crowded place. More than seven million people living in a space half the size of Prince Edward Island. A far cry from the wide open spaces of Manitoba." She put a hand on Naomi's arm, then added, "And get ready for apartment life, my girl."

"I'm ready," Naomi shot back, grinning.

Sara smiled and gave her daughter's shoulders a squeeze. "Me too."

1

The young girl and her mother sat with their heads together at the window, and continued to look out over the lush, peaked islands of Hong Kong, surrounded by water that sparkled on a cloudless August day. The ocean was tranquil and calm, a sea of deep blue with shades of jade and streaks of turquoise.

"It looks sort of—Mediterranean, wouldn't you say, Mom?" Naomi declared as she looked at her mother with mischief in her eyes.

"You're right, I think. But how would you know that?" Sara responded.

"From your old photos," Naomi replied. Her mother had travelled across Europe one summer many years ago, and had always spoken of her love of the Mediterranean, and especially the islands of Greece. But Naomi knew her mother's favourite country—aside from her home country of Canada—was Japan. Naomi's mother had lived in Japan twice in her life: the first time, as an English teacher newly graduated from university, when she had gone to live in a small farming village on the southern island of Kyushu. It was in Japan that she had met Naomi's father, who was also a Canadian teaching English there. Fourteen years later Sara returned to Japan, to teach English on the northern island of Hokkaido. Only this time she was a struggling single mother, with a twelve-year-old daughter in tow—a daughter who desperately didn't want to be there.

Naomi cringed inside as she thought about those times—the days and weeks after her arrival in Japan. She had been full of bitterness and anxiety over being taken away from her friends, her grandparents, and her comfortable life in Portage la Prairie, Manitoba, a farming town on the Canadian prairie. She had resented being dropped into an alien culture, without being asked for her permission. For a long time, Naomi had nurtured these negative feelings and directed them all squarely at her mother, who was herself struggling to adjust to a new job in a foreign land.

Look how much time I wasted, fighting Mom about being in Japan, Naomi lamented, as the plane descended on its final approach to Hong Kong International Airport. But Naomi quickly cut short that line of thought. *Never mind. It's all water under the bridge,* she reminded herself as she pictured her dear grandmother, whom she called Baba, telling her this wise way of looking at past bad experiences. In time, as Naomi had discovered the delights of Japan and made new friends, she learned to love that wonderful country. And when it was time to return to Canada after a year, Naomi surprised herself by not wanting to leave! The year she had spent in Japan had been the most unforgettable year of her life.

As the plane glided towards the runway, Naomi sat in deep reflection, and her blue eyes darkened once again. *Then we went back to Canada and—*

"Welcome home!" Baba said through tears as she rushed towards Naomi and her mother. "Thank God you're home."

Naomi gave her grandmother a big hug before turning to the tall man beaming next to her. "Hi, Gigi—" she managed to say before her grandfather's strong bear hug squeezed the breath right out of her.

"We sure missed you guys," Gigi said as he put his hands on Naomi's shoulders. He then reached for a bag from the trolley he was pushing and placed it in Naomi's hands. With a puzzled grin, Naomi reached in and pulled out a small stuffed toy; a cartoon cat holding a banner that read 'Welcome Home'."

I know how much you like Garfield," Gigi said. "Your stuffed toys have been missing you. They're all still on your bed—right where you left them a year ago. I'm sure your grandmother dusted them off—"

"Oh?" Naomi said. She had completely forgotten about her prized collection of stuffed toys. It had been so long since she had given them any thought. She could feel her face becoming red as she looked at the stuffed cat in her hands, and was surprised by the embarrassment she was feeling. "Thanks—"

Grandpa raised his eyebrows, then cleared his throat. "You know, there are two girls running around this airport somewhere, looking for you—"

"Naomi! Naomi!" someone shouted. Naomi whirled around to see her two best friends running towards her.

"Imee! Lois! What are you doing here?" Naomi cried out as she ran to them. The three embraced amid delighted squeals. Other passengers and greeters stopped to look at the happy young girls, and smiled at their exuberant and noisy reunion.

"Your Gigi brought us here, as a surprise," Imee said.

"We begged him to," added Lois.

Naomi draped an arm around each of them. *"I missed you guys so much—"*

"Tell us about Japan, Naomi. It sounds really interesting," Imee said.

"It is. And I will," Naomi replied, *"I met the most amazing people there. My friends Midori and Kiyoka and Ai—there's so much to tell..."*

"Hey everyone! Let me show you how to write your names in Japanese. It's so cool," Naomi said, sitting with a group of girlfriends at the Main Street Cafe. *"There's a special Japanese alphabet especially for foreign loan-words called* katakana—*"*

"Okay, enough lessons, Naomi. School's out for the summer," someone said. Everyone began to laugh. Naomi laughed too, a little, but her cheeks burned with humiliation. One of the girls brought up the name of a boy she liked, and from there everyone at the table launched enthusiastically into the topic of boys. Naomi listened to her friends' girlish giggles as they talked, and realized that she was not interested in the conversation. She issued herself a silent reminder that perhaps she would be just as boy crazy if she hadn't been in Japan for the past year. She felt strangely out of place and told herself to look interested if she wanted to fit back in with her old friends. Soon she found herself listening to the latest gossip about some of the older teenagers in Portage la Prairie, and what movie was playing in town...

"Gigi, did I ever tell you about sumo wrestling?" Naomi asked. *"It's such a bizarre-looking sport, but the Japanese love it!"*

Naomi's grandfather laughed and shook his head. *"Naomi. You sure do love that place. I'm just glad you came back when you did. Otherwise, who knows if you would have ever returned! I've got some work to do. I'll tell you what—why don't you come down to the hardware store with me like you used to."*

"No thanks, Gigi," Naomi replied, trying to hide her disappointment. *"Some other time..."*

"*All you want to talk about anymore is Japan!*" Lois said simply one day as the three friends were walking along Main Street. The girl stopped and put her hands on her hips. "*You know, there's a lot of interesting things happening here in Portage, if you'd care to notice—*"

That hurt. A nervous smile played across Naomi's lips.

"*Give Naomi a break, Lois,*" Imee cut in. She turned to Naomi, looking apologetic. "*I—we—like hearing about Japan. And your Japanese friends are great—*"

"*Sorry,*" mumbled Naomi. Her stomach felt crunched up and her arms felt heavy. She wondered if she had been talking too much about Japan. How could that be? Couldn't they understand how much the experience had meant to her?

"*I'll call you later,*" Lois said. Naomi and Imee watched as the girl ran across the street and into the library.

"*She's just a little jealous, I think,*" Imee said as they stared in the direction of the library. "*I think she thinks you're just not as happy to see us. Ever since you got back, you've seemed so wrapped up in Japan...*"

<hr>

"*Mom, sometimes I think my friends seem bugged about the fact that I lived in Japan. It's like, after the first day or so, their eyes kind of just glazed over, or something, when I tried to tell them about Japan. I don't get it. They all said they wanted to know, and I have a lot to tell—*" There were tears in Naomi's eyes. "*Things have changed, Mom. I came back and things are different now. They've changed.*"

Sara patted her daughter's hand. "*This is a common thing, Naomi. I remember when I returned from Japan the first time, and I was invited to my old school to talk about my experiences. I remember going back to that old school in Portage. It was so different from what I had remembered it to be; the ceiling seemed so low, the halls so narrow. What had seemed so big to me when I was a girl was really a very tiny place.*" Sara chuckled softly. "*But it's not really about how big you grow—it's about how you think. It's a wonderful experience to grow up in a small town—I did it. But you've had a very different experience, now, Naomi. Because of it, you see things differently. Actually, Naomi, it's not your friends who have changed—you've changed."* Sara paused, then added, *"You know what they say: You can never really go home..."*

Naomi shifted uncomfortably in her seat. *You can never really go home.* The words echoed in her head. *Go home?* she wondered. *Where's home? Returning home to Canada had been as much of a culture shock as moving to Japan—*

Suddenly, Naomi's thoughts were interrupted by a series of bone-rattling bumps. The plane began to shake and bounce. Naomi instinctively grabbed the armrests and looked around the airplane. For a fleeting moment she didn't know where on earth she was. Then Naomi looked out the window and instantly remembered that she was arriving in Hong Kong. The plane was speeding down the runway and Naomi found herself looking up at a wall of steep hillsides, covered in dense green bushes and trees. The plane had landed and Naomi hadn't even realized, so wrapped up as she was in her private thoughts.

She looked at her mother and smiled weakly, then reached over to give her a hug. Naomi felt she needed some reassurance. "I'm glad we're here—together," she said at last.

Naomi's mother laughed with surprise. "Of course we're together. We're the intrepid travellers from Portage la Prairie, and we'll be together for as long as you want, Naomi. Then, one day—a long time from now, I hope—I'll be an old 'empty nester', and you'll be off on your own to some far-flung corner of the planet," Sara said, and lightly kissed her daughter's forehead. "But right now, Naomi, it's time to start our Hong Kong adventure!"

Naomi smiled, grateful for her mother's enthusiasm, because at this moment, Naomi felt she needed it more than ever. As Naomi turned to look out the window to get a close-up glimpse of her new home, she reminded herself: *As long as Mom and I are together, it doesn't matter where we go.*

Wherever you may go, go with all your heart.

—Chinese Proverb

"Welcome to Hong Kong International Airport," the flight attendant announced, then proceeded to explain about the customs and immigration area, the baggage claim area, and modes of transportation into central Hong Kong.

"We don't need to know about that right now," Sara said, now sounding a little weary after the twelve-hour flight from Vancouver. "A colleague from our school will be waiting for us."

As Naomi and her mother stepped off the plane, they were enveloped in hot, steamy air. Naomi had never felt anything like it. "Whoo!" she gasped, as the humidity settled in her hair and on her skin. Naomi and her mother filed into the terminal building, instantly grateful for its air-conditioned comfort, and followed the crowd up an escalator. They looked at each other quizzically when a few of their fellow passengers began to hasten towards the row of immigration officials. Soon some of them began to run, prompting others to do the same. Naomi saw one man in a business suit sprint to the shortest line, and she giggled. After picking up their suitcases and clearing customs, Naomi and her mother passed through glass doors into the spacious arrivals hall, where a large crowd was gathered. Many people were pressed up against the guard-rail, looking anxious. Some were holding name cards. It was a noisy place.

"Over here, Naomi," Sara said, and pushed her trolley towards a young Chinese woman holding up a sign that read: *Sara Nazarevich.* The woman smiled and reached out to shake hands.

"Welcome to Hong Kong, Sara. And you are Naomi, right? I'm May Wong, one of the teachers at the Hong Kong Canadian School."

"Hello, May. Nice to meet you. And thanks so much for coming to meet us. I'm not sure what I would have done, this place looks so big and—"

"Awesome," Naomi finished, looking up in wonder at the enormous airport terminal building.

May smiled. "Yes, this airport is the biggest in the world—for now. But we are always outdoing ourselves here in Asia. It's actually quite easy to get around. Follow me, the airport shuttle is just over there. I've already bought the tickets."

Naomi followed May and her mother out the exit to a train platform. People were bustling all around: scores of families pushing trolleys piled high with suitcases and boxes, men and women walking smartly with only a briefcase in hand—even groups of people who looked like they had no particular place to go, but rather had come just to watch the excitement. A shuttle train approached the platform and, as the doors opened, Naomi quickly stepped aside to avoid being bowled over by the wave of passengers.

Already a little disoriented due to jetlag, Naomi's head started to spin. "People sure seem to be in a hurry here," she commented.

May laughed. "This is nothing. Just wait until you get into the streets of Central on a weekday at lunchtime."

Naomi wanted to know what May meant, but was too tired to ask. *I guess I'll figure that out sooner or later,* she thought to herself. *For better or for worse, I'm here for the long haul. And this time it was my idea.* Naomi pushed her suitcase into the luggage rack and, after motioning to her mother that she didn't mind sitting alone, took a seat by the window behind the two women. She let out a long sigh and settled back, happy just to let the landscape speed by for the next 23 minutes, until they arrived in Hong Kong's Central district. As Naomi allowed herself to relax, she felt a twinge of anxiety begin to emerge from the pit of her stomach. Immediately Naomi tamped it down. *This is not Japan—and*

I am not a wimpy 12-year-old. I'm 15 years old and we're in Hong Kong. Because of me.

Naomi reminded herself that she was the one who had first spotted the job ad in the newspaper in Winnipeg—the one announcing jobs in Hong Kong for Canadian English teachers. Naomi had kept the ad in her desk drawer for several days before showing it to her mother and broaching the subject of her mother applying for a job. Sara was surprised that her daughter was in favour of the idea, although she herself was very interested in the opportunity. Both Naomi and her mother had heard much about Hong Kong, especially since 1997, when Hong Kong, until that time a colony of Great Britain, was peacefully handed back to China. Naomi had done a lot of research about the former colony, now referred to as a 'Special Administrative Region of the People's Republic of China' for a school project, and was captivated by what she'd discovered.

It hadn't taken Naomi much to persuade her mother to apply. Naomi told her mother that she was up for the adventure, and that she had learned a lot about herself during her year in Japan. Naturally, her grandparents were not so keen, but they were well aware of the adventurous spirit that their daughter and granddaughter shared. After a telephone interview and a medical examination, Sara was offered a position at the school and soon Naomi and her mother were wrapped up in a whirlwind of activities: selling their meagre few pieces of furniture, buying new suitcases, deciding which things to keep for the trip and which things to ship—and which things to put in storage in Gigi's barn, buying airline tickets, getting a series of inoculations, and making arrangements to enroll Naomi at the school. It was almost June before Naomi began to tell her friends and teachers that she and her mother would be leaving again for another adventure in Asia.

And now, we're finally here, Naomi thought, as she looked at the skyscrapers of Hong Kong Island, from the ground this time.

"Did you hear that, Naomi?" Sara asked as she peeked at Naomi from between the two seats. "May says our apartment is in an area called Happy Valley—isn't that cute? It's near a racecourse. And May says we have a harbour view, too. That'll be lovely!" Naomi's mother sounded excited and happy. She gave her daughter a big grin before turning back to chat with her new coworker.

Naomi looked at the top of her mother's head, and watched it bob merrily as her mother laughed and talked with May. *We're finally here. This was my idea. And we're going to have another big adventure,* Naomi told herself forcefully. Naomi remembered the admiring looks when she'd told her classmates and teachers that she was moving to Hong Kong. The idea seemed to impress everyone. *I'm lucky to be able to live all over the world,* she told herself.

"Harbour view?" Sara asked, her voice tinged with disappointment. Naomi and her mother were standing in the middle of the living room in their new apartment in Happy Valley. Scattered around them were the suitcases and carry-on bags they had brought from Canada, and a few bags of groceries and house-cleaning items that the school had thoughtfully provided. After a quick tour to show Naomi and her mother how to use the gas stove and the water heater, May had left, promising to be back on Monday to take them to the school to get settled in, before classes started the following week.

Naomi walked over to the window, noticed that it was in need of a good cleaning—the whole apartment was—and surveyed the sea of buildings in front of her. "So that's the harbour view—right there in between those two highrises," she said, pointing to a narrow gap in the distance through which a sliver of water could be seen. Naomi pondered this for a moment, then turned to face her mother. "Well, we won't be in here most of the day anyway, will we? Besides, look at all the apartment blocks around here—this is obviously one thing about apartment living that we'll just have to get used to," she said, trying to sound cheerful.

Sara brightened. "You're right, I suppose. It's no big deal. Let's check out the rest of our new home."

The two stepped over their bags and went to Naomi's bedroom. Naomi walked in and looked out the window at the same highrises she'd seen from the living room. Then, grinning at her mother, Naomi stood next to the narrow bed and proceeded to try and touch both sides of her bedroom at the same time. The room was so small, Naomi was almost able to touch the opposite walls, and she made funny grunting noises as she tried. She grimaced as she pretended to stretch herself beyond her capability. Naomi wanted to make her mother laugh and it was working.

"Naomi stop. Stop!" giggled Sara. She sat down on the bed and giggled some more. "I'd call this room rather cozy—wouldn't you say?"

"Oh, yes! 'Cozy' is definitely the word I'd use," Naomi replied.

Sara stood up, cheerful once again. "Great! Let's see if my room is any bigger than this one. Maybe I'll be nice and we can flip for it."

"Really?" Naomi asked, and she grabbed her mother's arm.

Sara laughed, "Oops! Sorry, Naomi. I was just joking."

"Oh, never mind," Naomi responded with mock disappointment as she entered the master bedroom. It was not much larger than Naomi's own tiny room. Sara peeked in over her daughter's shoulder.

"Okay—so this is it. Not so bad," Sara said finally. We'll start cleaning this place up tomorrow. For now, let's just get ourselves cleaned up, and then we'll go for a walk around the neighbourhood. Let's take it easy today."

Naomi nodded and headed back to her bedroom. She stood in the doorway and looked around silently for several moments. It was not much to look at. Naomi sighed, then walked over to her backpack. She unzipped a small pocket and pulled out a photo, which she placed carefully against the small lamp on the table by her bed. Naomi sat down on the bed and stared at the photo for a long time.

"My little baby half-brother. My brother," Naomi whispered. She had never met the boy. She'd seen her father only once since he remarried more than two years ago, just before Naomi had returned to Canada from Japan. Tears sprung to Naomi's eyes as she remembered being told the surprising news of her father's remarriage. *Why didn't you want me there?*

Naomi rose from the bed and stood in front of her bedroom window, determined to push such thoughts out of her mind. Her gaze swept across the expanse of highrise apartment blocks and commercial skyscrapers. Some looked grand and elegant, but many looked dingy and old. It was like a wall of concrete and glass—so different from the view from her home in Manitoba; a street of tidy, green front lawns and small square houses. *Nothing fancy*, Naomi thought, *but it was comfortable. What I see here sure doesn't make me feel very comfortable.*

And now, as the shadows lengthened over the Hong Kong skyline, Naomi allowed herself to think the truth. It was a truth she knew had always been there, but one that she just didn't want to know. The real reason behind her wish to come to Hong Kong was not a simply a quest for adventure and travel to exotic places. It was as much a desire to leave things behind. And, lately, Naomi felt she was in danger of becoming rootless—some sort of lonely wanderer. She turned and stared at the photo again and thought about her father's new family and his home in Toronto. *Here's to home—wherever that is,* Naomi said in an imaginary toast to herself. *I'm taking a chance, here—hope it works.* Ever since she returned to Canada after her year in Japan, Naomi had felt a little lost and out of place. Naomi often wondered if her mother ever felt the same way, but was always too afraid to ask.

The Chinese animal zodiac comes from the legend of the Jade Emperor of Heaven, Yuhuang Dadi. One year, he invited all the animals of Earth and Heaven to celebrate his birthday, but only 12 came: the Rat, Ox, Tiger, Rabbit, Dragon, Snake, Horse, Goat, Monkey, Rooster, Dog and Pig. For such loyalty, he honoured each animal with a year of its own. From that day, people have assumed the nature of the animal in whose year they were born.

—Star Signs, Love Signs, by the Mystical Madame Li

N aomi open her eyes, and saw that it was only 6:30 in the morning. She grimaced. The air-conditioner wasn't coping well with the heat and humidity, and the apartment smelled slightly musty. Naomi rolled over and looked up at the ceiling, feeling hot. *Monday morning—again. A new school—again.*

Sara stuck her head in the door and smiled. "Ready for the big day?"

"Yeah," Naomi replied. She shrugged her shoulders, trying to shake off the heat that enveloped her. She wasn't at all convinced she was ready for anything.

Naomi headed to the shower. The water, barely warm, was a relief. *This weather!* thought Naomi. *Scary!* When she stepped out of the shower, the humid air attacked her once again. Beads of sweat gathered on her upper lip as she brushed her hair in front of the bathroom mirror. *Ugh! My hair feels sticky—and it's getting all curly.* Naomi rubbed out a clear spot in the middle of the foggy mirror and looked at herself. *My eyes are puffy.*

My whole face is puffy. She grimaced at her reflection, then sighed in frustration as she put on her robe and went to the kitchen for breakfast.

Later, as Naomi was putting on her new school uniform, she thought about her school, and the one she'd left behind. There was no comparison in terms of outward appeal. *The Hong Kong Canadian School is the best school I've ever seen,* Naomi thought. *But what about the students? I wonder what they're like.* Naomi remembered her mother's comment about being glad that school fees were waived for staff. She knew that school fees at international schools like this one were quite expensive. *They're probably all incredibly rich,* she said to herself, and felt a wave of self-consciousness course through her. Naomi knew that Hong Kong was a very unique place, where people from all over the world came to live for a time. Many were very wealthy. She remembered the exotic-looking people she had seen in the streets of Central district. *The students would be much more sophisticated than me—just a girl from Portage la Prairie,* Naomi guessed.

"Okay, Naomi," Sara called out a few minutes later. "We'd better get going." They stepped into the corridor and headed for the elevator. Naomi was a little rattled once again when the elevator doors opened to the lobby and the humidity descended.

"Whoo," Naomi said. She began to fan her face, then realized it was no use.

"No kidding," her mother replied. Another, stronger, blast of Hong Kong heat and humidity struck them both as they stepped outside. "Let's walk slowly. In fact, let's take a taxi."

"Good idea, Mom," Naomi replied gratefully.

Naomi and her mother walked gingerly down the block. Naomi shouldered her school bag and shook her head sadly, feeling the heat already seeping inside her clothes. She turned to look at an inviting little green space across the street and noticed a group of elderly people, standing in rows and doing a series of slow, synchronized movements.

"That's *tai chi,*" Sara commented.

"Hmmm," Naomi mumbled, and thought for a moment about the ballet classes she used to take in Canada, and the Japanese martial art of *kendo* that she had practised in Japan. She looked farther up the street. The taxi stand was getting closer, but there was a long line of businesspeople and uniform-clad students already waiting. *I'm going to be all sweaty by the time I get to school,* Naomi thought glumly, as she took her place at the end of the line. Naomi glanced enviously at a Chinese schoolgirl standing at the front. Within a minute, a taxi drove up and Naomi watched the girl reach for the car door. As she did so, she looked back at Naomi and shouted, "Want a lift?"

Naomi, startled, did not reply.

"You're going to the Hong Kong Canadian School, aren't you?"

Naomi checked herself. *Our uniforms are the same!* Naomi grinned at the girl and looked at her mother. "I've got my mother with me," she called back.

The young girl smiled and motioned with her arm to get in. "That's okay—where does she want off?"

Naomi and Sara scurried to the taxi. "She's going to the school, too," Naomi said.

"New teacher?" the girl asked, then looked anxiously behind her. Another taxi was pulling up behind theirs. She slid over to the far side of the seat and said. "Come on. Let's go. Can't keep anybody waiting."

Sara and Naomi slid into the back seat beside the girl, and the cab sped off.

"Thanks for the ride," Naomi said and, as she relaxed in the cool comfort of the air-conditioned taxi, she added, "This is great. I thought I'd melt out there."

The girl smiled again, "I thought you might be new. I've never seen you waiting for a taxi before. This weather is nothing. It's September now. You should be here in July and August."

"As bad as that? We're in trouble then," Sara replied. "It's not very humid where we come from."

"Where's that?"

"Manitoba—that's in Canada. Have you ever heard of it?" Naomi answered.

"Oh, yes. I'm from Canada, too," the girl replied, then added, "At least, now I am. I lived in Vancouver for four years. We left here just before the Handover in 1997—but we're back now."

"What grade are you in?" asked Naomi.

"Ten. That's Form 4 here in Hong Kong. What about you?"

"Same," Naomi replied with a grin.

The girl grinned back, "I'm Jovita. You can hang around with me, if you want."

"Thanks, Jovita," Naomi said. "I've never heard that name before. Is it Chinese?"

Jovita laughed, "Hardly. My mother gave it to me when I was little. She wanted me to be *joyful* and *vital*," she said, emphasizing the two words. "My Chinese name is Sin Lam. A lot of people here give themselves English names when they are in school, if their parents don't do it for them. It's a very Hong Kong kind of thing to do."

Naomi and her mother nodded.

Jovita continued with a grin. "Most names are pretty normal, I guess. But some of the names people choose are quite strange. You'll see. There's a girl at school named Circle—and a girl named Apple, too!" She laughed and leaned over towards Naomi. "My father works at a big company, and every time a new employee starts, their name and picture are posted on the bulletin boards. He says he looks at those notices to get a laugh, sometimes. He's seen photos of a Human, a Potato—and a Radio!"

"No way!" Naomi said, incredulous.

"I'm not kidding! Anyway, here we are," Jovita said as the taxi pulled up in front of the school.

Naomi could see throngs of students walking up the hill towards the school. Nerves started to tickle her stomach and she was glad that Jovita had offered her the ride, so that she didn't have to walk in alone. Jovita raised her arm to flag down a friend, then turned to Naomi and said, "You coming?"

Naomi looked at her mother and smiled. "See you after school, Mom. I'll stay with Jovita and her friends for lunch."

Sara smiled at her daughter mischievously. "Want a hug?"

"Later, mom," Naomi replied. "Have a great first day of work." She waved and walked into the school with Jovita and the other girl.

After an easy morning of orientation in science, French and art classes, Naomi spent the lunch hour with Jovita and her talkative friends, including another Canadian girl named Caroline. Naomi didn't say much, but listened as her new friends chattered away, recounting their summertime adventures. It was fascinating listening. A girl named Ming had spent her summer in Canada with relatives in Vancouver and Toronto.

16

Another girl told of being forced to spend three weeks at a Shakespeare camp in England. "At first I was mad. I didn't want to go," the girl, Sharon, said. "But it was fantastic. The best!"

"We went to Disneyland—again," said Mandy, and rolled her eyes. "It was because of my little brother. But I got to go shopping in Beverly Hills and that was the best part."

Jovita said, "Mom and Dad took me to Nepal just a couple of weeks ago. We went hiking in the Annapurna." She leaned forward, and the entire table of girls leaned forward as well, listening intently. "But it's the wet season. Leeches everywhere! And the mountains were obscured by clouds the entire time. I did get a nice shot of Mount Everest, though—" she paused, then added, "from the airplane window." The girls giggled at Jovita's misfortune.

"Bad *feng shui*, Jovita. That sounds like really bad *feng shui*," Mandy said, stabbing at the ice cubes in her glass with a straw. She turned to Naomi. "What did you do this summer?"

Naomi sat up, caught off guard. She was wondering what *feng shui* meant, but was not about to let her ignorance be discovered by these worldly girls. *My summer vacation sounds so boring compared to theirs,* she thought. Naomi took a deep breath for courage. "Well, I knew I was coming here, so we—my mom and I—spent most of the summer on my grandparents' farm."

"Where's that?" Caroline asked.

"In Portage la Prairie—in Manitoba. You've probably never heard of it—"

Ming cut in. "I know where Manitoba is. I fly over it every time I go to visit my aunt and uncle."

"Tell us about the farm, Naomi. I've never been on one," said Sharon. "What kind of farm is it?"

Naomi looked around the table, and saw that all eyes were fixed on her. "Well, I help out on the farm—mostly in the garden. Vegetables. Corn, carrots, beans—all that. My grandfather had big fields of wheat and potatoes, too. Usually, in the summer, my friends and I go swimming in Lake Winnipeg. We like to pick strawberries and raspberries, too. We have barbecues—"

"Mmm. Sounds great," said Ming, "My uncle in Toronto had barbecues almost every day when I was there. I wish we could do that here."

"Yeah, I know," added Jovita. "No barbecues allowed on our balcony." Naomi noticed everyone around the table laugh and nod their heads in agreement. She laughed along with them, not knowing exactly where the humour was in Jovita's statement.

The conversation turned to boys when Mandy mentioned that she had broken up her boyfriend over the summer. Judging from the reactions of the girls around the table, it seemed to Naomi that this was welcome news. Everyone had something to say about the boys in their classes, as well as gossip about possible summer romances. Naomi listened in silence, wishing that she knew who they were talking about.

"Have you left a beau crying at the airport back in Canada, Naomi?" Mandy asked with an impish grin.

Naomi looked over at the girl. The smile on her face looked like a smirk to Naomi. "I didn't have one," she replied in a small voice, and immediately regretted it. It sounded so pathetic. There was an awkward silence around the table, and Naomi berated herself. *I could have said yes, and they wouldn't have known the difference,* she thought.

"Some of us don't have time for such things," Jovita jumped in with an air of mock disdain. The girls giggled.

"Yeah, sure, Jovita," someone retorted with a laugh. The others began to laugh too, including Naomi, and she felt grateful to her new friend for taking the pressure off. For a moment Naomi thought about her friends in Portage la Prairie—and how certain topics of conversation seemed universal. *Boys!*

Later that afternoon, as Jovita and Naomi found themselves sharing the same study period in the library, Naomi decided to ask her new friend about what she'd heard earlier.

"What was Mandy talking about, Jovita? What was she saying?" Naomi tried to remember exactly the words that Mandy had said at lunchtime. "Fung shooey?"

Jovita laughed, "*Feng shui.* You can just pronounce it 'fung shway'. It's a Chinese thing. Hmmm. *Feng shui.* How can I explain it?" Jovita grabbed Naomi by the arm and led her to an aisle of books. "I think it's time you learned the wisdom of the ancients," she intoned, pretending to sound like a teacher. "Chinese civilization is the oldest—and wisest—of all civilizations," Jovita continued, then laughed. "Really, there's a lot of interesting and fun things to learn from ancient China—you'll see. *Feng shui* is the biggest thing in California these days. Everyone—movie stars even—want to get in on it." Jovita looked slyly over at Naomi. "Although I don't suppose you'd know that, way over there in Manitobey."

Naomi guffawed and gave her cheeky friend a slap on the wrist.

"I think *feng shui* is pretty fascinating, myself," Jovita said, as she picked a book off the shelf and passed it to Naomi. "But it's also just a lot of common sense, if you ask me. For example: Putting a mirror in the front entrance of your home, facing the front door, is bad *feng shui*, because it doesn't let the good spirits in. Well, that makes sense, doesn't it? I mean, when you go to someone's house, the first thing you *don't* want to see is your own tired old face staring back at you, is it? And the idea of clearing things out of your home from time to time, in order to create a better energy—doesn't everybody do that anyway? You have to do that in Hong Kong, that's for sure, since the apartments are so small."

Without waiting for Naomi to respond, Jovita steered her friend to another aisle. "But—even better—are the ancient secrets of Chinese astrology." Jovita scanned the shelves, then grabbed a book. "This author—she's great."

Naomi took the book from Jovita: *Star Signs, Love Signs*, by the *Mystical Madame Li*. Naomi was intrigued. "What's it about?"

Jovita's eyes danced. "It's about Chinese horoscopes. It's about finding out what our true personalities are," Jovita replied, and added slowly, "And who is our perfect match." She giggled. "There's a guy in my class who I've had my eye on for a year. Gorgeous. Looks like a Canto-pop singer," Jovita confided. Then, noticing Naomi's blank expression, she added, "Cantonese pop-music singer." The girl shrugged. "Anyway, he's a Monkey—not my type, unfortunately, since I'm a Rabbit. We're doomed to incompatibility."

Naomi grinned. "Do you have one of these books?"

"Every year I buy one!" Jovita replied. "I'm a real sucker for this stuff. But I swear to you it's all true! Let's look up your sign—" Jovita began.

"I'm a Dragon," Naomi replied. "I learned that when I lived in Japan. I didn't realize that whole animal-horoscope thing was a Chinese invention, though."

Jovita stepped back for a moment, eyeing her friend, "A Dragon! Well, lucky you! Wouldn't we all want to be lucky like the Dragon." She looked at Naomi for a few seconds, regarding her friend with new interest, then stated matter-of-factly, "As I said, I'm a Rabbit, myself. Delicate and refined. Graceful. A born diplomat." Jovita smiled as she brushed some of her long black hair back over one shoulder, and assumed a model's pose. "That's me."

Well, that's certainly true, Naomi thought admiringly, as she regarded her new friend.

The bell rang, signalling the end of the period and the end of Naomi's first day of school in Hong Kong. She turned to replace the book on the shelf, but Jovita stopped her.

"If you don't sign out this book, I'm going to sign it out for you," Jovita said with a grin. "Now you can read up on your *loooove* signs. And remember—the wisdom of the ancients," she intoned.

They were both giggling as Jovita left the library. Naomi headed towards the check-out desk, then went over to wait in front of the staff room for her mother. Naomi and her mother took a bus home, and spent the entire time talking and listening to each other's news of the day. They hardly noticed, as they arrived at the lobby of their apartment, that the door was being held open for them by a man who'd arrived at the same moment. As they all entered the elevator together, Naomi and her mother were still so engrossed in their conversation that neither of them pushed the button to take them to their floor.

"Sounds like you've already met some nice girls, Naomi—"

"Which floor?" the gentleman asked.

Sara and Naomi looked up at him. "Oh—" Sara began, then looked over at the panel of lights. The man had already pressed the sixth floor button. She raised her eyebrows and smiled. "I guess we're neighbours."

The man smiled slightly and turned back to face the elevator doors. Naomi watched him as he looked up to watch the numbers light up one by one. The elevator became silent. Naomi looked over at her mother and noticed that she, too, seemed to be focused on the stranger. A bell rang, and the man held the door open for Naomi and her mother.

"Bye, now." Sara said to the man, as she stepped out into the corridor.

"Cheers," the man replied, and walked off in the opposite direction.

As Sara searched her purse for the key to the apartment, Naomi turned to look down the corridor at the man. At that same moment he stopped at his doorway, turned his head to Naomi, and smiled. Embarrassed to have been caught observing him, Naomi quickly turned to face her own front door, pretending that she hadn't noticed his friendly smile.

four

The charming Goat is a pragmatic and adaptable character. People find the Goat, with its unassuming ways and gentle manner, easy to get along with. This is a good thing for the Goat, who prefers companioship over solitude. The Goat is sensitive and spiritual, attuned to the beauty all around it— in nature and in life.

Famous Goats: Michelangelo, Mark Twain
—Star Signs, Love Signs, by the Mystical Madame Li

L et's see if that old man and his friends are in the park, Naomi decided. She had been playing with the idea of going to the park to watch the old people doing *tai chi.* Naomi was eager to try it. It had been more than a month since Naomi arrived in Hong Kong and she was feeling a little restless. In Canada, Naomi had studied dance, and in Japan she had studied *kendo,* which she loved. But there seemed to be no ballet schools or *kendo* lessons available nearby. She put on shorts and a T-shirt, splashed her face and brushed her teeth, grabbed her backpack, and closed the door quietly behind her.

Naomi could see the familiar group of elderly people as she reached the park. Naomi headed to a nearby bench, and the old man smiled at her. Naomi smiled back, watching with interest as the group practised a series of graceful movements. Sometimes the old man stopped and turned to face the group, explaining something in Cantonese and demonstrating a position, while the rest of the group watched. Naomi could see that the old man had a cheerful and dignified air. When he spoke, it seemed that the others were listening to his words with great respect and attention. The man turned to face the front once again, and everyone attempted to try what appeared to be a new manoeuvre. Some people faltered, and clapped their hands with a grin, before they tried to regain the correct stance in harmony with the rest of the group. People were smiling at each other encouragingly. *It seems like a fun, peaceful way to spend each morning,* Naomi thought. *I wonder if I can sign up for lessons somewhere.*

"Hello! Hello!"

Startled, Naomi looked over at the old man again, who was calling and waving at her to join the group. Everyone was looking at her. Some were smiling and pointing for her to stand among them, in a space they had made for her. Naomi grinned and bowed her head, then put down her backpack and trotted over to stand among them.

"Good morning. I think you like *tai chi,*" the old man said. "Please come and try." He said something in Cantonese and once again turned to face the front. Naomi watched as the group began a routine and tried hard to follow them. It was difficult for her to keep control of her arms and legs, as the others seemed to do with relative ease. To Naomi, it felt as if they were all moving too slowly. Several times Naomi had to put her foot down in order to steady herself, or she would have fallen to the ground. Naomi admired everyone's easy sense of balance. *These old folks are putting me to shame,* she thought, and grimaced at her own lack of co-ordination. Several minutes later, the old man turned around and clapped his hands. Everyone relaxed and cooled down, shaking out their arms and legs. They smiled encouragingly at Naomi. The group began to break up and Naomi returned to the bench to retrieve her backpack.

"Thank you," she called over her shoulder.

The old man looked at Naomi. "You are welcome to join our group whenever you want," he replied. "Although you would be the only young one. I don't know what kids these days do. They are not so interested in old-fashioned things, like *tai chi,* I think. By the way, my name is Chen."

Naomi smiled, but remained silent. She wasn't sure if she wanted to join a group of old people practising *tai chi* in the park, even if it was so early in the morning that no one her own age would ever know. Naomi had to agree with the old man that people her age would probably not be doing such a thing. *Well, maybe I am different.* Naomi thought. In any case, she wasn't sure how to politely refuse the offer. "Okay," she said, "I'd like to try it for a while—on Saturday mornings, if you don't mind."

"Not at all," Chen replied. "You would be most welcome."

"Thanks, Mr. Chen—" Naomi began.

"Just call me Chen. That will do," he replied.

"Okay, then—Chen. Thanks. I'll see you next Saturday at 7:30—if I can get up that early,"

Chen's eyes twinkled, and he replied, "We start at 7:00. Every day unless it rains."

With a satisfied smile, Naomi left the small park and headed back home. The elevator door opened and Naomi stood motionless with surprise. In front of her stood her mother and the man from down the hall. Each had a different expression on their face.

"Well, your daughter hasn't done a runner after all," the man said with a grin. He looked from Naomi to her mother and laughed. He was dressed in tennis whites and had a racket-case slung over one shoulder.

"So I see," Sara said as she glanced at Naomi, then looked over at the man as he headed out the front door. "Have a good game, Steve," she called. "And thanks for the offer."

"Will do," Steve replied with a wave.

Sara turned her attention to her daughter and said gravely, "And you—young lady who can't even leave a note when she disappears in the night—get in this elevator."

Naomi knew from her mother's tone that she was in trouble, but she felt indignant about being talked about as if she were a child—and with a total stranger, too. Naomi tossed her head in the direction of the front doors. "Steve, eh? And what has he offered to do for you?"

"I bumped into him as I was coming out of the apartment. I told him you had disappeared and that I was going to look for you. He offered to help." As the elevator took them to their floor, Sara continued, "His name's Steve. He's British. From Yorkshire. Lives in 604." She turned to face her daughter, the smile gone. "You know, Naomi. I really was worried."

"Sorry, mom. I'll leave a note next time. But I'd appreciate it if you wouldn't talk about me to strangers—and don't over-react, either," Naomi finished shrilly. The more she thought about it, the more annoyed she became. "I was just down the street," she added sullenly.

Sara put a conciliatory arm on her daughter's shoulder. "Fine, sweetheart," she said, "But will you at least tell me what you were doing so early in the morning? I'm all ears."

Naomi looked up at her mother. "I was doing *tai chi* in the park this morning. While you—I'm sure—were still in bed dreaming."

Surprised, Sara asked, "You mean with that group of older folks in the park?"

Naomi nodded. "Yes. I was just watching, really. But as I got up to leave, the old man invited me to join them—and I thought, 'Why not?' Actually, I'd like to find some lessons somewhere around here. I think there's a community centre nearby—I'll check it out." She giggled. "*Tai chi* is hard! It's not easy to control your body—to move so slowly."

"I can imagine," Sara said, turning the key in the lock. "I think it's great that you like to go out like that and try new things. I'm proud of you. Just leave a note next time—"

"Fine," Naomi cut in. "You don't need to make a fuss." *I can't believe mom asked that man—Steve—to help find me*, Naomi thought indignantly.

"Okay, Naomi. In any case, like I said, I'm glad you're showing an interest in things here," Sara said, eager to change the subject. "So, Naomi, I have an idea for the day. Let's go over to Mid-levels. There's a street there called Hollywood Road that is apparently filled with interesting little Chinese antique stores and places like that."

"Sounds like a plan, Mom," Naomi replied, just as eager to diffuse the situation.

Within the hour, Naomi and her mother were stepping off a bus in Mid-levels on Hollywood Road. Naomi followed her mother down a street lined with small Chinese restaurants, housewares shops, and several art galleries. Sara turned the corner and glanced up both sides of the narrow street. "Let's go this way first."

Naomi and her mother made their way slowly up the street, which was crowded with shop after shop of delights. Most of them were selling Chinese antique furniture or reproductions, as well as works of art from all across Asia. Naomi marvelled at the variety of exotic items, as well as treasures that reminded her of Japan. There were bronze and wooden Buddhas of all sizes; some were fat and happy, others were thin and gaunt.

Farther down the street, another window full of Chinese artifacts caught Naomi's attention. Beyond the store-front display, Naomi saw lovely Chinese brush paintings on the walls. She stepped inside the silent shop, which appeared deserted. As Naomi neared the counter at the back of the shop she heard footsteps in the back room, and looked up as a man entered from behind an old curtain. Naomi gasped. It was the man from the park—the man who had invited her to practise *tai chi* that very morning. He threw his head back in surprise, smiling brightly.

"Well hello," he said, "Nice to see you again."

Sara walked over to them and Naomi explained, "Mom, this is the man who does *tai chi* in the park."

Sara leaned across the counter and shook his hand. "Nice to meet you. I'm Sara."

"I'm Chen," the old man smiled, and turned to Naomi. "And I should have asked you sooner—who might you be?"

Naomi was suddenly struck by the man's excellent English. "I'm Naomi," she replied.

"This is a lovely shop," Sara said. "The art—everything—is lovely. Where does it all come from?"

"Thailand, Myanmar, Vietnam. But mostly the Chinese mainland," Chen replied. He waved his hand towards the wall next to him. Naomi looked at a felt banner festooned with an assortment of red and gold pins. "These Chairman Mao pins, of course, come from China. They are very popular with the tourists."

"Cool," Naomi stated, as her eyes travelled over the wide assortment of Mao pins, all with the face of the famous former leader of China, Chairman Mao Zedong. "But I'm not a tourist. I live here," she was quick to add. She was surprised by the hint of defensiveness in her voice.

"Oh, I know," Chen replied with a smile. "We've seen you standing at the bus stop every morning on your way to school."

After browsing in the shop a little longer, Naomi and her mother said goodbye to Chen, and as they walked down the narrow streets of Mid-levels, Naomi thought about the idea of coincidence—how she should come to meet Chen twice in the same day.

五

Chung Yeung Festival is on the 9th day of the 9th lunar month. Legend tells us that during the Han Dynasty, a man saved his family from destruction at the hands of roving bandits by taking them to a mountaintop along with food and a jug of chrysanthemum wine. A lovely autumn tradition comes from this legend: we go hiking and picnicking in the mountains on this day, and we visit family gravesites to pay respects to our beloved ancestors.

—Hong Kong Tourist Authority

On a Saturday morning in mid-October, Naomi, Sara and May were waiting in line at the Lo Wu border checkpoint with China. It seemed to Naomi that, on this day, everyone in Hong Kong wanted to get through the gates to China. "Where's everybody going?" she asked. It was sweltering in the immigration hall and Naomi was beginning to feel dizzy.

"They're all going home, wherever that may be. We're only going as far as Guangzhou—a couple of hours from here by bus," May replied. She was jostled by someone standing in the line beside them, and bumped into Sara. "Sorry, Sara," May mumbled. "It would have been easier to fly, but I always come this way. You must find this ordeal awful."

Naomi looked around at the sea of faces. She could tell that many people were impatient to get through the border crossing, but many more seemed to be waiting with a resigned and stoic patience.

"It's like this for all the main holidays," May continued. "But *Chung Yeung* is one of the more important ones."

Sara waved her hand. "Don't worry about us. We're just happy to have the chance to visit China with an expert guide."

May smiled. "I often make this journey to visit my grandmother. But, as I said, it's especially important to come during *Chung Yeung*—to visit the graves of our ancestors. I come alone, now. My parents feel too old to make this trip, but they insist that I make the journey to see my grandmother, who's almost 80 years old. My grandfather passed away years ago, and now my grandmother lives with my uncle and aunt. I have a few cousins in Guangzhou, too. You'll meet some of them."

"How did you end up in Hong Kong, then, if most of your family is in China?" Naomi asked.

May nodded. "Actually I was born in a town near Guangzhou. But we—my mother and father and I—came to Hong Kong in the mid-sixties, when I was small. It was a tough time in China for people like my father, who owned his own business. It was only a small factory that made plastic flowers, but it was successful, and he was targeted."

"The Cultural Revolution," Sara commented knowingly.

"That's right," May said, and continued, "It was an upheaval of society—a madness—that lasted for many years, until Chairman Mao Zedong died in 1976. But we were lucky. We came to Hong Kong early, before things got really bad. My father knew that we could be in danger, so he quietly handed his factory over to the local government and came to Hong Kong. I don't remember much, I was so young." May took a long breath. "My aunt and uncle, who chose to stay behind, didn't suffer very much, since my father had given his factory away to the state. But there were times—" her voice trailed off.

Naomi listened with keen interest. She had heard about the Cultural Revolution in school, but had never met anyone who had lived through it. Although May had been a small child at the time of the Cultural Revolution, it was clear to Naomi that the woman had been deeply affected by it.

All at once May brightened and she said dismissively, "Things are better now, in any case. Chinese people have become good at not dwelling on the past."

Fifteen minutes later, they were exiting the immigration hall and May lead the way to a row of buses bound for Guangzhou. "Don't be afraid to use your elbows," May called out as they struggled to get through the crowd.

At first, Naomi simply followed in May's wake. But she soon realized, as people on both sides of her began to push forward, that she was in danger of being separated from her mother and May. Naomi began to push her way forcefully through the crowd, determined to be just one step behind. It wasn't easy.

"Whew, we made it," said Sara as they boarded a bus.

"Okay, we can sit back and relax now," May replied, and let out a sigh. As the bus pulled away, May began to tell Naomi and Sarah about the big Chinese city of Guangzhou. "Guangzhou is the capital of Guangdong province. The British used to call it 'Canton'." May grinned at Naomi and Sara and added, "Guangzhou is known as an exciting city, compared to Beijing—the boring northern capital of China. Guangzhou has a reputation for being a rough and dangerous place. The people are considered aggressive and noisy."

"I think we're getting used to it," Sara laughed, and turned to Naomi, who was just relieved to be in her seat on the bus, safely removed from the crowds outside.

Later, at lunchtime, a waiter scurried to the table, balancing a tray piled high with round bamboo baskets and dishes of food. He placed them all on the table in a casual, noisy manner and quickly retreated. Naomi looked around the cavernous Chinese restaurant and could see that it was filled with customers busy eating and talking. The atmosphere was lively and friendly, but almost too noisy for Naomi's ears. *May wasn't kidding about the noise*, Naomi thought to herself, and then turned her attention to the food. Except for a plate of spring rolls, Naomi couldn't recognize anything. Everything seemed to be cut into small pieces or wrapped up in little parcels.

May poured some Jasmine tea and explained about the food in front of them. "We're eating *dim sum*, meaning 'light snack'. But, when you look at how it is written in Chinese characters, it literally means 'touch the heart'." May laughed. "I guess everyone knows that the way to someone's heart is through their stomach." May's family; her grandmother, aunt and uncle, and two cousins, began helping themselves, passing the plates and baskets of food around. Everyone was talking in Cantonese, but they would all look over at Naomi and Sara with interest to see what the two thought of *dim sum*.

"Try this, Naomi. It's a shrimp dumpling," May said.

Using her chopsticks, Naomi gingerly lifted the dumpling to her mouth and popped it in whole. With her mouth full, Naomi smiled her approval.

May explained, "Cantonese cuisine is highly admired, and Guangzhou is a city famous for its food. In fact, we have a saying in Chinese: To be born in Suzhou, to live in Hangzhou, to eat in Guangzhou, and to die in Liuzhou."

"Why's that?" asked Sara, reaching for a fluffy white bun from one of the baskets.

"Well, Suzhou and Hangzhou are both lovely places. Suzhou is supposed to be filled with lovely women," May replied. "And Hangzhou has a lovely lake. Both are not too far from Shanghai." May passed a plate of white-coloured squares to Sara. "Turnip cakes?" she asked encouragingly. "And Liuzhou—hmmm." May turned to the others at the table and spoke in Cantonese, which brought forth a discussion and laughter from her family.

"Liuzhou is famous for its coffins!" May declared. Naomi smiled, wondering whether her mother's startled expression was due to the odd fact about Liuzhou—or the taste of the turnip cake.

After lunch, May took Naomi and Sara to an enormous book shop. Naomi was entranced by the large posters of stern-looking men that adorned the length of one wall. Naomi felt they must be rather important people. "Who are they?" she asked May.

"Famous Communists," May replied. She pointed at the bushy-bearded man on the far left and began to name them. "Marx, Lenin, Stalin—I'm surprised they still have *his* picture up. And that big one is Chairman Mao Zedong, of course," May said, pointing to the face that Naomi recognized. "He's Zhou En Lai. That's Deng Xiaoping—he died only a few years ago. Hmmm. Over there's Ho Chi Min—he's Vietnamese, but a good 'comrade', as we say. May motioned for Naomi to follow her. "Some people think those posters are collectors' items. In Hong Kong there are vendors who make quite a brisk trade with the tourists selling stuff like that—and this," May added, pointing to a counter piled high with green army caps adorned with red stars, as well as two large porcelain bowls filled with red and gold pins.

"Mao pins!" Naomi exclaimed. I've seen these in a shop on Hollywood Road."

"Oh, so you know about them," May said. She chose a pin, then stuck it on Naomi's collar. "There you go, Naomi. A Mao pin for you. Every good Communist should have one. Or at least every good tourist. A nice souvenir from the People's Republic of China."

Afterwards, everyone headed by bus into the nearby countryside to visit the grave of May's grandfather. Naomi watched as May and her two cousins lovingly swept the area surrounding their Grandfather's grave. May's uncle helped his ageing mother lay some food at the grave. Then May lit some long, thin incense sticks and stuck them into a sand-filled pot in front of the photograph on the gravestone. Everyone bowed their heads in silence for a few moments. Naomi couldn't help thinking how differently things were done back in Manitoba. She thought about funerals in Canada, and realized she had never even been to one.

"My family is going to return to Guangzhou now. But we are going to go on a hike up there," May said, and pointed to the hilltop over her shoulder. "My grandfather used to love to go up there. And it is part of the *Chung Yueng* tradition. I make this climb every year." The three shouldered their packs and headed across the area of gravesites to the edge of a field, where the trail began. "It'll take about an hour to get to the top. Don't worry though, the hill is not that high."

"Lead the way," Sara replied with enthusiasm. Despite the heat, Naomi was eager for the walk. She was glad to be out in the countryside, and hadn't realized how much she missed being out in nature. As they crested the hill, they realized they were not the only ones enjoying a hike; several families were picnicking at the top. May shrugged and set down a blanket, then began pulling a few small bags of food out of her backpack. Soon, they were all enjoying their snacks and basking in the welcome October breeze.

On their return to the Guangzhou bus station two hours later, Naomi noticed a small crowd gathering by one of the platforms. As she rose in her seat to get a better look, Naomi froze. She could see what appeared to be a young woman standing at the centre of the crowd. She was bent double, clutching her stomach. She lifted her head for a moment and Naomi could see that the woman's face was contorted in pain, and she was reaching to steady herself against a vending machine. An older woman came forward to try and help and Naomi could see the younger woman pushing her away. Then Naomi looked down at the young woman's feet. Blood. Naomi was horrified.

"Mom—"

"Okay, Naomi. Someone is coming to help her. Let's go." Sara, already standing in the aisle of the bus, put her hand on Naomi's shoulder.

Naomi looked over at May, who's face registered both concern and anger. "Don't worry, Naomi. She'll get the help she needs." May turned to Sara and said under her breath, "I can imagine what has happened. Poor girl."

"What's happened, May. Tell me," Naomi said. Naomi looked out the window again and saw two uniformed people breaking into the small crowd.

May looked uncertainly at Sara, then turned to Naomi. "I don't know for sure, of course, but big cities like this, they are a magnet for unfortunate young girls. They get pregnant, and they come to big cities for abortions. Many are done in secret. The abortions are dangerous—the conditions are dirty—each year many women die." May sighed. "It happens often. The girl comes to the city for an abortion, and dies from the consequences when she gets back home. At least that girl may have a chance—she didn't get on the bus home yet."

May shook her head, looked from Sara to Naomi, and continued, "Life is not easy for girls in China. There is a saying created by the Communists: Women hold up half the sky. But our Chinese culture and traditions run deeper than that. There is another saying in China, that girls are like bathwater—easily thrown away. It is not very lucky to be born a girl in China, especially in the countryside, I think. Boys are preferred, since they can better help out in the fields, and also, it is the boy who carries on the family line. So when a girl is born, it may be unwanted. The unwanted baby girl will—if she's lucky—be left at an orphanage." May paused. "That's if she's lucky. But many new-born girls are killed. There is even a special term for this—in English we call it 'female infanticide'."

"I don't think we need to hear any more," Sara said quietly. Naomi saw her mother look over in the direction of the stricken young woman, and could see the fear in her eyes.

Naomi didn't want to believe what she had heard. For a moment, Naomi wished she was back in Manitoba. *People don't talk about things like that there, she thought. It seems so unfair—that girls should be treated so cruelly, just because they are girls. What's so special about boys, anyway?* she asked herself. For an instant the image of Naomi's half-brother entered her head. She shook it loose.

Not much was spoken on the bus back to Hong Kong. By now, all three were tired from the long day. The hike, as well as the disturbing scene they had witnessed at the bus station in Guangzhou, had put them all in a sombre mood.

Naomi and her mother were exhausted when they arrived at their apartment building. They waited impatiently for the elevator, watching the numbers light up on its way down to the ground floor. When the doors opened, Naomi was face to face with the man they'd encountered earlier. He looked at Sara and Naomi, who were by now looking quite forlorn and dishevelled, and smiled. "Nice day for a hike," he said, as he headed for the door.

Sara managed a weak smile but Naomi said nothing. She just wanted to shower and get into her safe, comfortable bed. Later that night, the image of the stricken young woman at the bus station kept creeping into Naomi's mind, and she thought about what May had said about the plight of unwanted infant girls. It was the last thing she thought about before she finally fell into a restless sleep.

Our Mission Statement: We endeavour to give loving care to babies and children as they await their new homes, and to help young women dealing with crisis pregnancies.

—Mother's Love

N aomi lay in bed and stared at the patch of sky through her bedroom window. The mornings were starting to get a little darker. She noticed, also, that the humidity was beginning to lose its edge, and was grateful that she had made it through what everyone assured her was the worst of Hong Kong's heat and humidity.

No snow this Christmas, that's for sure, Naomi thought. Everyone says the weather will be lovely in December, when Baba and Gigi come to visit. Naomi smiled up at the calendar on the wall by her desk, and giggled at the thought of her grandparents walking through the noisy, crowded streets of Hong Kong. *They won't believe what they're seeing,* Naomi thought with a grin. *Baba and Gigi have never been further west than Saskatoon—and now they'll be coming to China!* Naomi began to think about their planned trip to Beijing as well. *I'll finally get to see the Forbidden City, and Summer Palace—and the Great Wall of China. I can't wait—more adventures.*

It's been only two months or so, and we've got a nice life here, Naomi reflected with satisfaction. *Mom's got a good job. She's happy. I've got some friends and a nice school. Hong Kong's way different but I can handle that.* She surveyed her little bedroom: her bed, a wardrobe, a desk piled with books and papers. Naomi looked out the window again. She could see the morning sun reflected in the windows at the tops of the highest buildings.

'The world is your oyster' Baba had once said. "And it is," Naomi whispered. *Mom and me—we'll be fine,* she told herself. Then, Naomi stood motionless for a long while. *Why do I tell myself that?* she pondered. *Do I really mean it?* She focused her gaze at the highest building in front of her, the top of the Central Plaza tower, and forced herself to be truthful: *Sometimes when I say it, it's because I believe it. And sometimes when I say it, it's because it's what I need to hear.* Naomi shrugged with annoyance. These conflicting feelings were rising up to confront her more often than she liked in recent weeks, especially since the trip to Guangzhou. The image of the young woman at the bus stop entered Naomi's mind again. Naomi shook her head to try to get rid of it, and wondered what she could do for a diversion.

It was a Sunday. She wanted to see where her mother was, and whether she had any interesting ideas for the day. Naomi found her mother seated at the dining table writing something down on a blank sheet of paper. There was a pot of tea, two cups, and a plate of toast on the table. Sara looked up at Naomi as she entered the room.

"Morning, sleepy girl," Sara said.

"What's up, Mom? What's the plan?" Naomi asked as she slid in the chair next to her mother and reached for a piece of toast.

"Funny you should say that. I am making a plan," Sara replied as she put down her pen. "Since you've started *tai chi* lessons with your friend Chen, it got me thinking." Sara took a sip of her tea. "I should be doing something too. I'd like to participate in the community in some way."

"I think that's a great idea, Mom. I love my *tai chi* lessons. It makes me think I am doing something to understand Hong Kong—and China—better," Naomi said, as she dripped a spoonful of honey on her toast.

Sara smiled as she looked at the generous dollop of honey her daughter was about to enjoy. "I'm glad to hear that, Naomi. There's so much to know about this place. Hong Kong is such a modern metropolis, but it's also part of a very ancient culture."

"No kidding," Naomi added. "So many contrasts—things that surprise you. This place is so different from Manitoba."

Sara thought for a moment. "It's good to have a kind of coping strategy when you move to a new place—especially a place as different as Hong Kong!"

"Well, it's working for me," Naomi said. "It worked for me when I was in Japan, too, when there were no ballet classes—so I decided to learn *kendo*."

Sara nodded approvingly, "It's too bad that you can't take up *kendo* here in Hong Kong, but it sounds like you are going to get a lot out of your *tai chi* classes with Chen. I have been thinking of what I can do. I've been thinking about it for quite a while." She took another sip of tea, then put her cup down and stared into it for a few moments. "The thing that happened—what we saw—at the bus station in Guangzhou last month really got to me. It made me think of something I've had in my mind for a long time—long before we came to Hong Kong." She looked up at Naomi. "You know I like to work with kids—"

"You like to work with kids? Whew, that's a relief. You're a teacher aren't you?" Naomi interjected with a grin. She was eager to hear what her mother had to say, and what her coping strategy was going to be.

"Funny girl—that's right," Sara said. She wrinkled her nose and waved off her daughter's joke before becoming serious once again. "Actually, Naomi, I'd like to spend some time on weekends with other kids. May mentioned there's an orphanage and shelter for pregnant girls over in Mid-levels, near Hollywood Road."

Naomi put her cup down, and sat up in her chair. It was not at all what she expected to hear. "You want to work weekends at an orphanage?" she asked.

Sara waved her hand, "Oh, nothing as formal as that. I'd just go in and volunteer. Apparently they encourage people to come in to play with the children on a regular basis." Naomi noticed that her mother's eyes had a faraway look.

"That sounds like a fantastic idea, Mom," Naomi said, intrigued.

Sara looked over at her daughter with a grateful expression, and then patted the table. "Well, I'm glad you think so. With your gaggle of girlfriends, and now with *tai chi* lessons, you'll have plenty to do on weekends, so I thought I'd like the company over there. Anyway—we'll see." She added, "I'd like to go over there later this morning, just to check things out. Do you want to come along?"

"Sure I'll come along," Naomi replied. She thought her mother's coping strategy was a fascinating idea. And she was more than a little interested in seeing what a real orphanage looked like.

Naomi and her mother caught the bus to Mid-levels. They got off near Hollywood Road, then Sara stepped into a shop to ask for directions to the orphanage. Naomi watched her mother and the shop owner through the storefront window. Both were talking, gesturing, and nodding vigorously. Naomi smiled. *I've seen that all before,* she thought. *That's how you communicate when you can't understand the language.* Naomi followed her mother along a steep, narrow street lined with tiny Chinese restaurants, a few art galleries, and assorted small businesses. "Number 38. Mother's Love. This is the place," Sara announced with triumph, "I knew we were close." She and Naomi were standing on a narrow sidestreet, staring up at a three-story brick house. Sara looked up at the old house, which seemed out of place between two commercial sites; a real-estate agency and a dry-cleaning shop.

There was a look of doubt on Naomi's face. "This doesn't look like an orphanage," she commented, and then reminded herself that she had never before been to one.

Sara held the door open for Naomi, and they stepped into a Spartan-looking foyer. Two worn wooden benches lined one wall, and above them hung a poster, neatly framed. Sara and Naomi walked over to take a closer look at the poster, a stylized drawing of a woman holding a baby. Naomi's gaze rested on the text beneath the drawing.

"It's their mission statement," Naomi heard her mother say.

Naomi read the words and looked at her mother. She could see that her mother was staring intently at the poster. Sara's face held an expression that Naomi couldn't figure out and was sure she had never seen before.

"Mom?"

"Are you here to see someone?"

Naomi and Sara turned around. A woman, who had been sitting behind the reception counter at the opposite corner of the foyer, and had not been visible from the front door, was now standing and looking at the two visitors with a pleasant smile on her face.

"Actually, I'm interested in volunteering. I'd like to spend some time with the children here," Sara began.

The woman turned to speak with a colleague behind the counter, then soon emerged from behind a nearby door. She walked over to Naomi and Sara and shook hands. "Welcome to Mother's Love. My name is Edith Leung."

"Hello, I'm Sara Nazarevich. This is my daughter, Naomi. We've just moved to Hong Kong from Canada—"

There was a flicker in Edith's warm expression. She asked, "You have not been here long? How are you finding things in Hong Kong? Of course, there are the standard complaints. Although they are from everyone here—not just the expatriate community."

"You mean the pollution and the crowds?" Naomi asked.

Edith nodded, her eyes merry. "Yes—and the prices. Hong Kong used to be known as a good place for bargain shopping. Not anymore, I'm afraid."

They all laughed. It was well known that Hong Kong was perhaps the most expensive city in the world.

"How long do you intend on being in Hong Kong?" Edith asked. "Here at Mother's Love, we require our volunteers to commit in a long-term way." She continued, apparently searching for words, "I'm sure you understand—about the idea of commitment. It's better for the children."

"Oh, I do," Sara quickly replied. "I can't say exactly how long I'll—we'll—be here. But for the time being I'm working here as a school teacher on a two-year contract. I can assure you that I understand the need for commitment and consistency. I was thinking of volunteering once a week—"

Edith brightened, "Well then, let me show you around and tell you about our organization. I've been here since the beginning." She waved her hand around the foyer. "As you can see, our premises are small. And, strictly-speaking, we are not an orphanage, since some—most, in fact—of our children have been given up for adoption. Mother's Love is more like a home rather than an institution." She led Sara down a corridor and Naomi stepped in behind them. "We have all sorts of people who come to spend time with our children. Couples, singles—most any age. Even a few teenagers." Edith smiled at Naomi. "All we ask is that our volunteers spend time here on a regular basis, over a lengthy period. We don't know in advance how long our children stay with us, but while they are in our care we want to give them the chance to develop relationships with the volunteers." Edith stopped at the stairwell and turned to Sara. "Actually, it's hard on the volunteers when the little ones eventually leave us."

Sara nodded. "I can imagine."

They walked up a flight of stairs and headed down the corridor. There were three playrooms, each devoted for children of different age groups. Naomi and Sara peeked in a small room and saw a young woman sitting on the floor with three crawling babies. Naomi was enchanted by the cozy little group of rosy-cheeked faces and shining black hair. It was clear to Naomi that the woman was really enjoying herself at Mother's Love. They peeked in another room to view a group of toddlers, and then Edith showed Naomi and Sara the dormitory rooms and the bathroom and changing area. The place was simple, but clean, and Naomi could see that the children were well cared for.

Edith began to lead Naomi and Sara back down the stairway to the front foyer. "We have guest rooms on the top floor. That's where the young girls stay." Edith pointed to the ceiling. "We provide counselling for the pregnant women—girls, really—and their families. In some cases, however, the families do not wish to be involved. We usually have one or more young girls living here for the duration of their pregnancy. During an adoption, we also provide a room for the child and their adoptive parents. In such cases, they all stay here together for a few days before the children finally leave Mother's Love for good."

Sara and Naomi nodded. Naomi looked up at the ceiling, and wondered if there were any girls living up there at that moment. *Pregnant girls,* Edith had called them. *Girls in trouble,* that's what Baba and everyone back in Portage would call them. Naomi thought about one girl in high school back home who had become pregnant. *Or at least, that's what the rumours said,* Naomi thought. The girl hadn't returned to school the following September. *But I didn't know her myself,* Naomi thought. *I don't know anyone whose ever been pregnant—unless they were grown up and married. Things like that don't happen—not in my sheltered little world.*

"Well, I hope you've enjoyed the tour. It's always a pleasure for me to meet people who are interested in volunteering. But it is a serious commitment," Edith said. She reached behind the counter, pulled out a brochure, and handed it to Sara. "Read this about Mother's Love—and about our two affiliated orphanages in China. Think about it for a while. We look forward to hearing from you. Being a volunteer at Mother's Love is a rewarding experience." She shook Sara's and Naomi's hands and escorted them to the door, waving from the top of the stairway.

Sara started walking down the sidewalk with her eyes on the pamphlet, and Naomi silently fell into step behind her. Naomi and Sara had walked half a block down the street and had stopped at the street corner before either of them spoke.

"Well, Naomi, that was very interesting. I'm really glad we came," Sara remarked, as she continued to ponder the information in the pamphlet. Naomi could see the thoughtful, enigmatic look on her mother's face, and she wished she could read her mother's mind. Naomi watched as her mother carefully tucked the pamphlet in her handbag and put her hands on her daughter's shoulders. "Listen, Naomi, I'm starved. Let's find us some lunch. Remember, Sunday is a good day for *dim sum*."

The highest truth cannot be put into words. Therefore the greatest teacher has nothing to say. He simply gives himself in service, and never worries.

—Chinese Proverb

N aomi jumped out of bed, pulled on a pair of jeans and a T-shirt, grabbed a pair of socks, and headed to her mother's bedroom. Sara turned towards Naomi with one eye open, the other still fused shut with sleep.

"I'm off to the park to see Chen," Naomi whispered.

Sara sat up in bed, "Great. I'll be going over to Mother's Love at about 9 o'clock. If you don't have plans, why don't you meet me there at 11:30, and then we can do some sightseeing over on the Kowloon side of the harbour. We can go to the bird market or the jade market—or a temple."

Naomi nodded with enthusiasm. "Good idea. We need to scope things out—" she grinned, "so we know where to take Baba and Gigi when they get here."

Sara looked up at the ceiling and laughed quietly. "No kidding. I'm sure my Mom will be so surprised when she sees some of the typical Chinese markets. They're definitely not like the superstores back home."

Naomi couldn't help smiling at the thought. "See you later, Mom. Bye," Naomi said as she went to the living room to look for her running shoes, and laughed to herself as she sat down and began to pull on her socks. She was imagining the look on her grandparents' faces as they walked through the bustling Chinese market in their neighbourhood:

everything—fish, chickens—dead and alive—were out in the open, in stalls that overflowed onto the streets. Enormous carcasses of raw meat, streaked white and red, hung on hooks. Loud vendors sat on their stools next to colourful piles of vegetables and fruits, offering samples. There always seemed to be action whenever Naomi passed by the market, and she thought it was a fascinating and lively place. *It's definitely not what Baba and Gigi are used to,* Naomi reflected with a twinge of anxiety. *I hope they'll have a good time here.* Naomi realized it would be her grandparents' first time outside of Canada since immigrating there from Ukraine when they were not much older than herself.

Naomi headed to the park and waved to Chen and the others as she passed through the gate. Several members of the group looked up and nodded or waved as they continued their *tai chi* routine, and one woman made room for Naomi in line beside her. As Naomi took her position among them, some of the old people said a cheerful, if a little self-conscious, morning greeting in English. It was clear to Naomi that they were happy to have her join their little group.

Naomi turned her attention to Chen, who was standing at the front, facing forward. She began to concentrate on emulating the old man's graceful and deliberate movements. Again, Naomi was struck by the surprisingly difficulty. It was easy enough, Naomi thought, to copy the arm movements, but when Naomi tried to focus on her legs, that's when things began to fall apart. Several times Naomi faltered and she stood to watch Chen and the woman beside her follow through on a particularly complex routine. Naomi blushed when the woman looked at her and laughed. But the old woman's smile was an encouraging one, Naomi knew.

"Naomi?" Naomi heard someone calling her name from a distance.

Naomi looked over at the street and saw Jovita and her brother heading up the hill. They were dressed in shorts and T-shirts and carrying badminton rackets. Naomi held up her hand in a silent greeting.

"What are you doing? We're going to the sports centre—want to come with us?"

Naomi stood quietly for several seconds, wondering what to do. For a few moments, she was tempted to leave Chen and the group of old people and go off with her friend. She could feel the smile on her face harden as embarrassment crept into it. It was almost as if she had been caught by Jovita and her brother, doing something she shouldn't be doing. After all, Naomi herself had never seen anyone her age doing *tai chi* in the park. She took a deep breath, and decided it didn't feel right to leave Chen and her lesson. *It wouldn't be polite to just pick up and take off— I've only just arrived. Besides, I really want to learn this stuff,* Naomi reminded herself.

"Thanks, but no. I'm taking my *tai chi* lesson," Naomi called out to Jovita.

Naomi could see Jovita raise her eyebrows in surprise, and then the laughter started. "So I see. I knew you were a crazy *gweilo!*"

Naomi laughed back. She could hear Chen laughing, too. "You're pretty crazy yourself, up this early on a Saturday," she retorted with a smile. Naomi knew what the word *gweilo* meant. It meant 'white devil' and reminded her of the term *gaijin*, which she'd heard in Japan. In both cases, it was a term used mostly for Western people, although the meanings were a little different. In Japan, *gaijin* means 'outsider'. When Naomi had first heard it, she had been quite offended. The term *gweilo* meant 'white ghost' or 'white devil' and originated many years ago when the Chinese and the Western invading forces were wreaking havoc in China. These days, the term *gweilo* — like *gaijin* in Japan — was a very common slang term that meant, more than anything else, simply 'foreign resident'. Naomi laughed at her friend's sense of humour, but even so, she felt a little uneasy about refusing Jovita's invitation. Naomi wondered if she needed to try harder to fit in with her own crowd.

Naomi returned her attention to her *tai chi* practise and it seemed all too soon that Chen and the rest of the group were winding down and preparing to leave. Naomi waved as the group filed out the gate, then went over to talk to Chen.

"Thank you for the lesson, Chen. Are you sure your friends don't mind that I am coming here every Saturday morning?" In a strange way, a little part of Naomi hoped that Chen would say yes—that he and his friends *did* mind that she—a foreign interloper—had joined their *tai chi* exercises. Then she wouldn't have to wonder if she was doing the right thing.

Chen's response cut into her confused thoughts. "On the contrary, Naomi. They look forward to your attendance. They are very pleased that you are interested." He turned and walked off to retrieve his gym bag propped up against the fence that bordered the park at the back. Naomi watched as Chen suddenly straightened his back and began yelling angrily in Cantonese, raising his arm in a threatening manner. Naomi froze, startled by the old man's unexpected outburst. Chen leaned over the fence, yelling into what appeared to be a concrete drainage area that snaked down the hillside. Naomi slowly walked over, almost afraid to discover the reason for Chen's invective. She heard some children's voices and some laughter, and then another loud volley of angry Cantonese from Chen. Naomi peeked over the fence and saw two little boys clambering up the side of the drainage ditch. She watched as the boys turned and taunted Chen, before climbing over the fence on the other side and disappearing between two apartment buildings.

Chen watched the boys retreat, then turned to Naomi, shaking his head with anger. "Those boys," he began, "I've told them many times to stay away from there. It's very dangerous." He looked at Naomi and pursed his lips. "I shout at them from my window over there," he continued, pointing to a small window on a building on the other side of the ditch. "It's always those same two naughty boys. They never listen."

Naomi followed Chen in silence as he grabbed his bag and went to sit on the bench. He was breathing heavily after the confrontation with the two boys. Naomi wasn't sure whether it was from anger or from the exertion of his shouting, which Naomi imagined was something Chen rarely did. To Naomi, Chen seemed like a quiet and dignified man. The two sat on the bench for a short while in silence. Naomi didn't know what to say.

"Well, I'm sure they won't ever come back, after what you said to them—whatever that was," Naomi said awkwardly after a time, to break the silence.

Chen looked over at Naomi and laughed softly. "I hope so. I gave them a talking to. And it wasn't the first time." He pointed his chin in the direction of the drainage ditch. "During rainy season, especially during a rainstorm, that ditch fills up fast." He waved his arm towards the slope beyond the ditch. "As you can see, Hong Kong Island is all hills. Things can get very dangerous when it rains. There are always landslides and floods to worry about." He pointed to the fence. "That ditch becomes a torrent. Just because it's sunny today and the ditch is dry—silly boys. They don't think." Chen looked down and shook his head silently. A few moments later, with a vigorous slap to his knees, he stood up and gave Naomi a smile. "Well—enough. We'll be seeing you next week?"

Naomi nodded, "I'll be here, Chen. I enjoyed the lesson. When I lived in Japan, I practised *kendo*. Now that I'm living in Hong Kong, I've decided that *tai chi* is something I'd really like to learn more about." She looked down at her feet for a moment, "It's kind of like my souvenir of living in Hong Kong. My Mom and me—we travel a lot. I've lived in a few different places in the last few years, and it's nice to have something to focus on, when you hardly know anyone—" her voice trailed off. She looked up and could see Chen looking at her intently through his smiling eyes.

Chen tilted his head and smiled, then pursed his lips. "You know, Naomi, *tai chi* isn't just about practising how to move your arms and legs—physical conditioning. *Tai chi* is a small part of a larger idea. It's part of a way of living—about how you think of yourself and your life."

Naomi nodded, trying to understand what Chen was trying to say. "My friend Jovita was telling me about how great ancient Chinese wisdom is—about things like *feng shui*, for example. I'd like to know more—" she began to say.

Chen nodded, impressed. "Ah, then you are learning about your energy—your *qi*. *Tai chi* can help you to balance your *qi,* especially at times when you feel 'unbalanced'—in your mind and in your thoughts," Chen said. He hefted his bag. "I must leave you now. I open my shop at 9:00 every day. I'm never late," he said with a chuckle. "If you are not busy later, come by."

"I will, Chen," Naomi replied.

As Naomi watched Chen leave the park, she decided to phone Jovita, to see if she could join up with her for the day, instead of meeting her mother. But Jovita had not returned home when Naomi called, so, after a shower and breakfast, Naomi took the bus over to Mid-levels and got off on Hollywood Road. She was feeling lonely, and thought she would do some window-shopping before meeting her mother at the orphanage and stop at Chen's shop along the way. Naomi loved walking down this street, oddly named for the famous movie district in Los Angeles. It seemed to Naomi that there were always new treasures to admire each time she came. Some of the art galleries, with their sparse decor—and which remained locked, only to be opened by a salesperson once a doorbell was pressed— looked too intimidating to enter, but other antique and bric-a-brac shops looked wonderfully mysterious and inviting. Soon Naomi found herself looking in the window of Chen's shop, which was, she thought, the most interesting and inviting shop of all. Naomi peered in towards the back of the shop and saw Chen behind the counter. With a smile, Naomi opened the door and went inside.

As Naomi drew closer in the darkened shop, she saw that Chen was lighting incense sticks. He carefully placed them in a small pot in front of two old photographs. Chen turned around and smiled at Naomi, then came out from behind the counter. He motioned for Naomi to take a seat on one of the pieces of antique Chinese furniture. Naomi sat gingerly in a strange-looking chair with a wide rounded back and a narrow seat made of interwoven lengths of rope. Despite it's odd appearance, the chair was surprisingly comfortable. As Naomi settled in with a smile, the chair creaked. She looked up at Chen with a worried grimace.

Chen laughed as he reached for a book on the counter and sat in the chair next to her. "Don't worry. These ones are reproductions. Made in Macau," he said with a laugh. He turned his attention to the book in his hands, which Naomi could see was old and well worn. "I'm glad to hear your friend Jovita is interested in ancient Chinese thought—Chinese philosophy. I didn't think young kids today cared about such things."

"Some of us do, Chen," Naomi replied.

Chen smiled and thumbed through the book. "China is an ancient civilization. There are philosophies that are very old—"

"Like Confucius," Naomi cut in. "Doesn't everybody know about Confucius?"

Chen smiled, "Yes, Confucius is one man who created a philosophy—a way of thinking about things. But there are others, too. Chinese philosophy is very different from Western philosophy."

"I can imagine it is. But in what way?" Naomi asked, intrigued.

Chen wrinkled his brow. "Hmmm. We look at things very differently. For example, the concept of 'self'—and of 'destiny', for example. Our place in the universe."

The tin bells clanged as the door opened and three people entered the shop. Naomi turned from them back to Chen. "It sounds very interesting, Chen. If there's a book that will help me figure out my destiny and where my place in the universe is, I'd sure like to know what it is," Naomi joked. She rose gingerly from the chair. "I'm off to meet Mom for lunch now. She's over volunteering at the orphanage down the street."

Chen nodded thoughtfully and went with Naomi to the door. Naomi walked a few steps down the street, then turned around and saw that Chen was still standing on the sidewalk, smiling at her. Naomi waved back at him, then crossed the street and headed towards Mother's Love.

The Tiger is a sensitive yet dynamic creature. It is blessed with magnetic personal power, and is often regarded as a protector or authority figure. The Tiger is capable of great love, and is not afraid to take risks in such matters—once the Tiger has set someone in its sights.

Famous Tigers: Karl Marx, Beethoven

—Star Signs, Love Signs, by the Mystical Madame Li

N aomi reached the door of the orphanage as another young woman arrived from the opposite direction. Naomi held the door open, and the young woman bowed her head in Naomi's direction as she entered the foyer. Through the doorway, Naomi could see her mother talking with Edith.

"Hey there, Naomi," Sara said when she turned and saw her daughter. Naomi could see that her mother was excited. Sara's eyes danced and her mouth was a wide grin; with that look, Naomi knew her mother had a lot to tell. Naomi giggled when she heard Sara say, "I have so much to tell you! But first, let's find lunch!"

Naomi and her mother decided on a small but busy Chinese restaurant just down the street from Mother's Love. Seating themselves at the only empty table, they ordered their food by pointing to some of the dishes they saw being served to other customers. Soon Naomi and her mother were feasting on big bowls of wonton soup. Their table was covered with dishes of chopped barbecued chicken, steaming green *bok choy* stir-fried with garlic, and bowls of plain white rice.

"Those kids are beautiful! Gorgeous! Like little living dolls!" Sara exclaimed in between slurps of wonton soup. "I barely know where to begin, Naomi—those sweethearts! I'm playing with a small group of one-year-olds—that's where I'll be for the time being. They are absolutely adorable!"

Naomi listened as her mother talked about her morning at the orphanage. There was something new about the look in her mother's eyes. *She's glowing,* Naomi thought, and found herself being caught up in her mother's enthusiasm.

"It sounds like you've found a great place to volunteer, Mom. The way you're talking about it, it looks like you are going to jump out of your chair! It makes me want to jump out of mine, too," Naomi said with a grin. Her mother laughed in response, and Naomi attempted to take a bite of meat from the large piece of chicken. She struggled, and the plastic chopsticks made a loud clicking noise as they lost their grip. The unwieldy piece of chicken and bone was left dangling from Naomi's mouth. She giggled and dropped the piece into her small rice bowl.

Sara burst into laughter. "How do they manage it?" she mused.

"You mean eating chicken with chopsticks? I have no idea." Naomi shook her head at the bowl of rice in front of her but then looked up at her mother with a serious expression. "Mom, do you think the orphanage would let me volunteer, too."

Sara's eyes widened. She put her chopsticks down and tilted her head. "I don't see why not, Naomi. But you have to commit to it. It's clear to me already how much my visits mean to those kids. It's important that you would be coming on a regular basis. Remember what Edith said?"

"Yes. I could handle that. My social calendar is not exactly full," Naomi replied, remembering when her mother had told her that she wanted to volunteer at the orphanage. At the time, her mother had mentioned the girl at the bus station in Guangzhou. Now, the image of that girl came back into Naomi's mind, and images of cute little faces that had so entranced her mother. "I think I really would like it—just like you do."

Sara smiled at her daughter. "I think you would, too."

As they finished their lunch, Naomi told her mother of her own adventures that morning: about the *tai chi* class and seeing Jovita, wondering whether she should join her; about Chen and how surprised she had been when he had scolded the two boys playing in the ditch; and later about what Chen had said about *tai chi* and Chinese ways of thinking about life and destiny. When they arrived back at their apartment building, Naomi and her mother were still busy discussing their adventures of the day. They were giggling as they exited the elevator and turned towards their apartment, but stopped when they saw Steve standing in front of their apartment door. He looked at them and smiled, looking embarrassed, then looked down at the piece of paper in his hand.

"Hello there Sara—Naomi," Steve said—a little nervously, Naomi thought. He was wearing tennis whites again. But this time his white T-shirt had the words: BIG FOUR OH! emblazoned across the chest.

"Nice T-shirt," Sara said, eyes smiling.

Steve looked down. "Oh, this. It's old. From last year." There was a pause. Finally he spoke. "I knocked on your door earlier but you weren't home, so I thought I'd leave a note," he said, offering up the slip of paper in his hand. "This is the note." Another awkward pause, then he smiled sheepishly. "But now I don't need it—this note." He looked at the paper and shoved it in his pocket, then pulled his shoulders back. "I was wondering if you two had any plans for Chinese New Year?"

No, not yet, Naomi thought. Chinese New Year was after Christmas, in late January—more than six weeks away. *We're still making Christmas plans for Baba and Gigi. It's way too early to think about Chinese New Year—*

"No, we don't," replied Sara quietly.

"Well, I'm renting a junk—and I'd like to know if you two would like to come?"

"You mean—a Chinese boat?" asked Sara.

Steve laughed. "Yes, well, not a real Chinese junk. They're called junks, but they are really just small yachts. They fit about 30 people nicely, although there won't be that many. Just some of my friends and co-workers and their families for an afternoon cruise," he replied. "And then I thought the three of us could go for dinner, and watch the fireworks together in the evening." The last statement ended up sounding hopeful, like a question.

"Oh—that would be great—eh, Naomi?" Sara replied happily, looking from Steve to her daughter.

Naomi paused for a few moments, and found herself forcing a smile. "Yes. Great."

Steve seemed pleased and relieved. "Great," he said to Naomi. He turned to Sara, then back to Naomi again. "Maybe you'd like to go out for dinner some time before then, too? Or have dinner at my place?" He grinned at Sara. "Just being neighbourly."

"What an offer! I'll certainly let you know when we're really hungry," Sara said with a laugh, and then immediately apologized for the gibe. "That was awful of me. It's just that an invitation like that is so rare. In fact, I can't ever remember getting one like it. I guess I just don't know any men who want to show off their cooking skills—but I'm sure you're a very good cook," Sara finished awkwardly and then, as she turned her key in the lock, she threw Steve a sidelong glance. "You *are* a good cook, aren't you?"

Steve laughed loudly. "British cuisine doesn't have the best reputation, I'll admit. But I can make a good roast beef—with Yorkshire pudding and mushy peas—"

"Mushy peas?" repeated Sara.

"A Yorkshire delicacy—although I suppose 'Yorkshire delicacy' is a bit of an oxymoron," Steve said as Sara started to laugh. "You might want to try them—mushy peas," Steve added, clearly pleased with how he had made his neighbour laugh. Naomi looked from her mother to Steve as they stood smiling at each other for a long moment. "Anyway, you're welcome anytime," Steve said finally, and headed back down the hall.

Naomi and Sara entered their apartment, and Sara closed the door behind her. She looked at Naomi with an odd expression. "A date?" she whispered, "A DATE? Did Steve just ask me out on a date?" She looked like she could not quite believe what had just happened on the other side of the door.

"It's just dinner at a neighbour's. And don't forget I was invited, too." Naomi declared, a little put off by the encounter—and by her mother's excitement.

Sara looked at Naomi and gave her a hug. "You're right. I know. But—it's been a long time, Naomi, since any guy—even the neighbour— has asked me—us—out to dinner."

Naomi silently regarded her mother's flushed cheeks and shining eyes, and a very strange feeling, like suspicion, crept into her body. It was a new feeling, an unsettling one. Naomi retreated to her bedroom and lay on her bed, then pulled out her history book for the distraction it offered. After a few minutes, she threw the book aside, and reached under her bed for the book of Chinese horoscopes that she had already renewed twice from the library. Naomi flipped through the book to the horoscope chart. *Steve's T-shirt was from last year, he said. So he's 41 now,* Naomi reasoned. She looked up his year of birth in the chart and scanned the column to the top of the page: *Tiger. Steve is a Tiger.* Naomi flipped through the book to the chapter about the Tiger personality. Naomi quickly skimmed through several pages and her eyes rested on one sentence.

"The Tiger's perfect love match is the Horse," Naomi whispered as she read. She grimaced, and let the book slide out of her hands to the floor. "Mom's a Horse," Naomi said to the ceiling. "Wonderful."

The telephone rang. Naomi jumped out of bed and raced to it. *I wonder who's calling? Hope it's Baba and Gigi. Hope it's anybody—for me.* "Hello?"

"Hi, Naomi? It's Jovita."

Naomi grinned. "Hi Jovita, what's up?"

"Are you free to make some plans for tomorrow. We're all tired of shopping, and want to do something strenuous for a change. I said you'd have a good idea—you're so sporty—*tai chi* with the old folks—and all that."

Naomi smiled at her friend's teasing. "Great! Hmmm. Something physical." Naomi paused. "Well, I'm the new kid here, but Mom and I went for a walk around the Peak a while back—"

"Yaaawn," Jovita responded.

Naomi giggled. "Okay then, I heard there's some rock-wall climbing overlooking the sea at a place called Shek O. Not sure where that is, though."

"Oh, Shek O. Lovely place. But rock-wall climbing is a bit extreme. Not for me, you understand—for the other girls," Jovita replied. Naomi could hear Jovita grinning at the other end of the line.

"Well then, there are some great hiking trails—"

"Yes, you're right," cut in Jovita, "and I've got the perfect compromise. "We'll walk the Dragon's Back and then take the bus to Stanley Market, followed by pizza. And then—shopping! That'll satisfy everyone. Thanks, Naomi! Just meet me at the bus stop at ten o'clock tomorrow morning. Don't be late."

"I won't, Jovita. See you later." Naomi put the phone down, suddenly very happy. She was grateful for Jovita's invitation and, in some way, she was relieved that she had someone other than her mother to spend time with tomorrow. The encounter with Steve in the corridor had thrown her off guard. She found her mother and said, "I'm going out for a hike tomorrow, and then to Stanley for lunch. I'm meeting Jovita at ten." There was a touch of defiance in her voice.

Sara looked up at her daughter and smiled, "That's great, Naomi. Sounds like fun." Then, with a sigh and a look of mock boredom, she added, "I guess I've just got my own company tomorrow."

Naomi looked down at her mother and put her hand on her hip. "Well, Mom. I know a man down the hall who might be wanting some company," she replied, then turned towards her room. She heard her mother's delighted laughter, but she herself was not smiling. It wasn't a joke. Naomi could feel anxiety in her stomach, and she regretted having brought up the topic of Steve. Naomi realized that whenever she bumped into him in the building or saw him in the neighbourhood, he was always alone. *Maybe he's a creep,* Naomi pondered. *I wish I hadn't given Mom any ideas.*

The next day, as Naomi and her friends were seated at a table eating pizza at Stanley Market, Naomi decided to confide in them about her neighbour. "There's a guy down the hall from us," she began, "Yesterday he asked me and my mom out for dinner. Yorkshire pudding and mushy peas, whatever that is. Sounds disgusting if you ask me."

Jovita laughed. "Oh yeah, I've heard of mushy peas."

Caroline added, "It's a British thing, Naomi. And pretty tasty, too."

Naomi nodded, once again embarrassed for having shown her ignorance in front of her friends, who seemed to know so much about so many things—including mushy peas.

"Never mind the mushy peas, girls. Naomi, did you say you and your mom?" Mandy asked in a shocked voice. "Sounds like bad *feng shui* to me."

The other girls groaned and Naomi laughed in spite of her anxious feelings. "He's Mom's age. He was really just asking my mom—I just happened to be there when he did it." Naomi looked down at her pizza. "But I think he's kind of weird. He's always by himself—"

"Maybe he's gay—" Ming said matter-of-factly.

A few of the girls giggled.

"If he was gay then why would he be asking them out on a date?" Jovita asked.

"Just being neighbourly?" Mandy said. They all laughed, except Naomi. She recalled that Steve had said those words exactly.

"It sounds like he is interested in your mom, Naomi," said Caroline. Naomi was not comforted by the excitement in her romantic friend's voice.

"Bad *feng shui*. Really bad *feng shui*," declared Mandy again. "I know what that's all about. My mom's had a few boyfriends in her time. But, I'm glad to say that my stepdad is a real sweetie—"

Naomi looked over at Mandy, who was grinning and rubbing her thumb and fingers together in the gesture for 'money'. All of a sudden Naomi's throat felt dry and her arms felt weak. "Stepdad? What are you talking about?" she cried out.

"Nothing wrong with stepdads, Naomi," Mandy said. There was a touch of indignation in her voice. Mandy sat straight in her chair, and lifted her chin. "My stepfather really *is* a great guy."

Jovita, eager to diffuse the growing tension around the table, interrupted. "Listen you guys, I'm full of pizza. Let's say we get going. I need to buy some Christmas presents—"

"Me, too," Caroline added hastily.

Talking ceased as the girls paid for the meal and headed out into the narrow alleyways of Stanley Market. Soon everyone was chatting about clothes and gifts, admiring the latest trends and the bargain prices. But Naomi couldn't think about shopping. All she could think about was what Mandy had said, and about the rift Naomi now felt between herself and that girl. Naomi was grateful for Jovita's and Caroline's thoughtful attention as they walked through the market, but Naomi could barely offer a smile in return, as hard as she tried to hide the turmoil that was building up inside her.

Stepfather? Naomi said the word over and over in her mind. It was unbelievable—and premature, Naomi knew, but the idea lodged in her head and made her fearful. She prayed that Mandy was wrong. Naomi had never given the subject any thought—she'd never had to.

That evening, Naomi told her mother she had eaten too much pizza and wasn't feeling well. Sara nodded sympathetically, and made her daughter a pot of Chinese tea to settle her stomach. Naomi took the tray and went into her bedroom, wanting to be alone. Naomi lay down on her bed and stared at the ceiling, not sure what to think. All she knew was that she was glad that Baba and Gigi would soon be in Hong Kong, and that they would be a family—the four of them all together—once again.

Welcome all tourists to Beijing! Formerly known as 'Peking', Beijing is the capital of The People's Republic of China. The population of Beijing and its environs is over 12 million people. Discover the ancient and modern delights this city has to offer! Visit the Palace Museum [Forbidden City] and walk in the footsteps of the Emperors! Learn about China's glorious past at the Museum of History and the Museum of the Revolution. Whatever your interests, Beijing has something for everyone!

—Beijing Tourist Authority

"Naomi! Look! Steve's come to see us off!" Sara said.

"I see him," Naomi replied. She tried to sound indifferent, but knew that she was sounding more indignant. *What's he doing here?* Naomi thought. *Just one more glitch in my plans for our great trip to Beijing. Things weren't supposed to be like this,* she lamented.

Only one week earlier, Baba and Gigi had called to say that they had cancelled their trip to China. Baba's best friend had passed away after a long illness, and Baba had decided she needed to be with the woman's family at this time. Naomi remembered the phone call; Baba had sounded very glum, but her spirits had managed to liven up a little when she'd asked Naomi about the mysterious neighbour. In her mind, Naomi heard her grandmother asking questions with an excited air: *So what's this fellow like? Is he a teacher, too? Have they gone out on a date?*

"Hi Naomi."

"Hi Steve."

"Are you ready for your big Beijing adventure?" Steve asked. He was carrying Sara's bag and reaching for Naomi's.

"I can carry it," Naomi said. She clutched her backpack possessively.

"This is so kind of you. What a surprise, getting this special treatment. I knew you worked at the airport, but it's such a big place, I didn't think we'd see you," Sara said.

"I don't work in the terminal building," Steve replied. "But I came here—I wanted to see that you two got off safely."

Naomi looked at Steve and her mother, and felt like the odd one out.

"Let's get going, Mom," Naomi said, trying to include herself in what was going on. "It's almost time to board."

Steve looked at his watch. "Oh, there's still some time—"

"Naomi, lead the way. I can't wait to go to Beijing!" Sara said with excitement. "It's too bad my folks couldn't join us, but we've planned a great trip. There's the Forbidden City, Tiananmen Square, Mao's Tomb. We even get to go to the Great Wall of China! It's not so far from Beijing—a day trip. And there's the Summer Palace—"

"I wish I could join you," Steve said. "I've lived in Hong Kong for more than five years and I still haven't made it to Beijing."

Steve walked Naomi and her mother to their boarding gate and waved as they boarded their airplane to Beijing. Naomi forced a smile as her mother waved back at Steve. Soon Naomi and her mother were ensconced in their seats on the plane, and Naomi was relieved to be alone with her mother again. She was sorry that her Baba and Gigi were not sitting next to them, but glad that Steve was going to be out of the picture for a week.

"Mom, can you just bend your knees a bit? I've got your face framed nicely by the Great Wall behind you." Naomi was looking at her mother through the lens of her camera, trying to get the perfect shot.

"Now, let's find someone who will take a picture of the two of us," said Sara. "A nice mother-daughter photo."

Naomi and her mother spent two hours at a restored portion of the Great Wall at Mutianyu, a busy tourist spot in the hills about 90 kilometres north-east of Beijing. But Naomi had discovered that, once they walked out some distance beyond where most of the tourists ventured, it was quiet and peaceful, and Naomi enjoyed being out in the bracing winter air. Beijing had proven to be as big and as bustling a metropolis as Hong Kong, although, with its flat landscape and absence of ocean, it in some ways made Naomi think more of Manitoba. From her vantage point on the Great Wall, Naomi looked out over a landscape of hills, lightly dusted with snow. She liked the way the wall—constructed more than two thousand years ago as a defensive line against northern invaders—snaked across the ridges and the crests of the hills. Naomi breathed in a lung-full of cold winter air. It was a welcome change from semi-tropical Hong Kong. *I wish I could just keep walking out along the wall and see where it leads me,* Naomi thought to herself.

Sara read her daughter's mind. "You go ahead, Naomi, but not too far beyond the restored section, okay? I'll just sit here and rest." Naomi smiled and nodded, then turned, almost skipping off farther along the wall.

Afterwards, Naomi and her mother wandered along the rows of shops selling souvenirs: carpets and quilts, T-shirts and coats, caps and fur-lined winter hats with ear flaps, as well as toys, carvings, and books. Naomi stopped to buy some postcards, then found an empty table at a tea shop. They gratefully rested their tired legs, and Naomi handed her mother some of the postcards as Sara ordered a pot of Jasmine tea. Naomi was surprised at how weary she was after the hike on the Great Wall, and welcomed the warmth of the shop. Naomi glanced over at her mother and saw that she was writing a postcard to Steve. At that moment, Sara looked up from her writing to notice her daughter staring at the postcard.

"Want to write something?" Sara asked.

"No," Naomi replied brusquely. "Why are you writing to him?"

"Oh, why not?" Sara responded. Naomi thought her mother sounded a little sheepish. "It was nice of him to see us off."

Naomi downed her small cup of tea and started on her own postcard to Baba and Gigi.

"How about finding a nice Chinese restaurant in your guidebook and trying some Peking Duck tonight?" Sara said after a while.

"Sounds good," replied Naomi absently, as she continued to write. She didn't look up at her mother as she spoke, and could feel her mother's eyes on her. Naomi knew that things were starting to get a little tense, and that it was because of her. She was sulking, she knew—and so did her mother. *But this trip was supposed to be another mother-daughter adventure, Naomi thought, and Mom's thinking about the neighbour. Naomi put her pen down and wrapped her fingers around her teacup, trying to figure out exactly what she was sulking about.*

Later that evening after an afternoon nap at the hotel, Naomi led the way up Wangfujing Road to look for their restaurant. It was a street not far from their hotel and only blocks from the famous Tiananmen Square. The street was lined with shops and restaurants of every description, and for every budget. Despite the winter chill, the street was crowded with tourists and locals who were out enjoying an evening where the action was. Naomi was caught up in the action and in a buoyant mood once again.

"I had no idea that China was like this," Sara remarked upon seeing the familiar red and yellow sign indicating a McDonald's restaurant. "One could almost think we were in North America."

"You're right," Naomi agreed. Many of the shop windows looked no different than those in Toronto or Vancouver. She noticed an assortment of restaurants along the street and felt her stomach rumble. "This is the place," Naomi said, as she glanced in the guidebook. "Best Peking Duck in town." Soon she and her mother were seated at a round table, looking hungrily at the assortment of dishes in front of them; strips of scallions, a plate piled high with thin crepes, and two dishes of *hoisin* sauce—a mixture of soybeans, garlic, chilli peppers and various spices. A waiter came up to the table pushing a trolley and lifted a large lid, revealing one crisply barbecued duck. Naomi watched the waiter deftly carve the duck into small slices and heap them on a plate. She could hardly wait to eat. The waiter smiled at Naomi and her mother and asked, "Do you know how to eat Peking Duck?"

There was silence, broken by Naomi's giggles. She had been quite surprised by the food on the table, having assumed incorrectly that Peking Duck was simply some kind of roast duck dish, eaten with the ubiquitous steamed rice. Naomi replied, "I'm not sure."

With a smile, the waiter took a crepe and spooned on some of the sauce. He then added a few pieces of the scallions and a few slices of the duck. Then he rolled up the crepe, placed it on a plate, and handed it to Naomi with a flourish.

"So this is Peking Duck," Naomi said. "Looks fantastic!" She reached for the crepe and took her first delicious bite of Peking Duck. Her mother watched with a grin and eagerly followed her daughter's example. Conversation stopped as they rolled several more crepes with scallions, sauce, and barbecued duck. Soon they were ordering another plate of crepes and more sauce as they made their way through the plate of duck. By the time the plate was empty they both had decided that there was no room for dessert.

"What a lovely meal, and it seems quite easy to make. I'll sleep well tonight," Sara said, patting her stomach.

The next morning was another early start. Naomi walked down the wide boulevard and soon found themselves standing beneath the large portrait of Mao Zedong at the Gate of Heavenly Peace—the entrance to the Forbidden City—at the north end of Tiananmen Square. They purchased guided tours on audio cassette and filed inside the enormous red-walled compound where the Emperors of the Ming and the Qing Dynasties lived and died—and rarely left throughout their lifetimes. Naomi couldn't comprehend the scale of the palace grounds; more than 40,000 rooms contained in hundreds of buildings. The compound also included a moat and, at the northern end of the compound, a 7,000-square-metre imperial garden, landscaped with rockeries and walkways leading over peaceful ponds to pavilions where one could stop to rest and admire the tranquil setting. Naomi was entranced, trying hard to imagine what the life of an Emperor could possibly be like.

After a quick lunch of noodles at a stand outside the north end of the Forbidden City, Naomi and Sara took a taxi to Mao's tomb at the opposite end of Tiananmen Square. They waited in line to enter the grand building housing the revered leader's embalmed body, which—in a custom that seemed reserved for the deceased leaders of Communist countries around the world—was on display. The line moved quickly, and as Naomi entered the eerily darkened room that contained Mao's body, she could see why: at the entrance and exit to this room stood four soldiers on guard. Inside the room, other uniformed officers quietly exhorted the people in line to keep moving along as they gazed upon the body of Chairman Mao. Naomi was speechless with awe and surprise as she shuffled in line. The only source of light in the darkened room came from within Mao's glass sarcophagus—the man's long-dead body laying on a plinth under a thick layer of glass. Naomi stared at Mao's familiar face as she walked slowly towards the exit. *It looks like him,* Naomi thought. *But is it really?* Naomi decided that his face had a suspiciously waxy, unreal glow to it, and she couldn't stop staring until she was out the door.

The crowd remained silent as they exited the chamber. Naomi shot a surprised look at her mother, who had sidled up beside her, and asked, "You okay?"

Naomi nodded. "I'm okay. Awesome. Unreal," was all she could say.

They wandered around Tiananmen Square, admiring the enormous statues of gorgeous men and women wearing uniforms depicting various occupations. Naomi saw a young peasant girl holding a huge sheaf of wheat in her arms standing next to a miner, a soldier, a nurse, a teacher, and others. All of them seemed to be looking intently in one direction, each with the same look of steely determination and pride.

"Ah, socialist realism," Sara said. "If only we could all look just like that—so handsome and strong and proud."

Naomi snapped a photo, then followed the group as they made their way to the bus taking them back to their hotel. Everyone was exhausted.

On the evening before Naomi and her mother were scheduled to fly back to Hong Kong, Naomi was on her bed, struggling to close her suitcase after packing it with the souvenirs she'd bought at the Great Wall, the Summer Palace, and at a market near their hotel. "Its good thing we're heading back to Hong Kong tomorrow," she said, sitting on her suitcase. "I have absolutely no more room in my bag." She grunted as she struggled to close the zipper, and thought about going back to Hong Kong. Despite the fact that Baba and Gigi weren't there, and the bad start the trip had gotten off to when Steve had come to see them off, the trip was everything Naomi had hoped it would be. But as her thoughts turned to Hong Kong, she began to feel a little anxious, wondering about what she would be going back to—all this new stuff between her mother and Steve.

"Steve! Hi!"

Naomi followed her mother's gaze towards the end of the corridor, and cringed inside. Again! Naomi thought. *Looks like someone needs to get a life. I wish he'd leave us alone!*

"Have you come to help us find our way again?" asked Sara with a laugh.

"I was just in the neighbourhood," Steve replied as he reached for her carry-on bag. He looked from Sara to Naomi, grinning. "How was the trip?"

"Fabulous, Steve."

Naomi stared intently at her mother, who was looking at Steve. Naomi noticed that her mother seemed a little bit more lively than she may have otherwise been after a long day of travel. Naomi sighed. She didn't want to think about what was going on between the two of them.

It was a quiet evening at home that night.

"Mom, why do you keep asking Steve to meet us at the airport?"

"I didn't, Naomi. He came on his own," Sara replied matter-of-factly. After a few moments, Sara added, "Why does it bother you so much, Naomi? You know, you hardly make a secret of it, if you ask me. He's a nice neighbour. Everyone should be so lucky—to be in a new place, and know that there are people you can count on."

Naomi didn't have an answer to that. She knew her mother was right, but she also felt that her mother wasn't being entirely candid. *But we don't need anyone,* Naomi told herself yet again, and wondered why her mother didn't see it that way, too.

The Ox is an individualist, with an ability to endure long hardships. The Ox personality is one of high morals and a quiet dignity, often making it difficult to ask for help. Because of this, the Ox tries to be self-reliant and conscientious. This extends to matters dealing with children: the Ox will do whatever it takes to ensure their children's survival and well-being.

Famous Oxen: Vincent Van Gogh, Nehru

—Star Signs, Love Signs by the Mystical Madame Li

On a Friday in mid-January, during a professional development day for Sara, Naomi found herself sitting at home alone, thinking about the date that her mother and Steve had gone on the night before. Naomi had heard her mother come in before midnight, and was hoping she would peek in to talk with her before going to bed. But her mother didn't do this. Naomi remembered feeling very alone—and she still did, worrying about this first date and the ones that were sure to follow. Naomi dreaded Chinese New Year, when she and her mother would have to spend the day together with Steve.

On an impulse, Naomi picked up the phone and called Baba and Gigi in Canada. Naomi hadn't spoken to them since she and her mother had called on Christmas Day. "Hi Baba! Did you get our postcard from Beijing yet?"

"Hello, Naomi. What a surprise! And we sure did. How was the rest of your holiday in Beijing?" Baba answered from the other end.

"Fantastic, Baba. So much to see and do. You and Gigi would've loved it—I think," Naomi replied.

"I think we would have, to. But we settled for a typical snowy Christmas—and a funeral," Baba said.

"I'm sorry, Baba—"

"We all are," Baba said softly. "I suppose it was just her time. She had a good, long life." There was a long pause before Baba spoke again, more cheerfully, "Tell me more, dear, about this fellow named Steve. Your mother has mentioned him a few times now. How does she really feel about him, Naomi—and how does he feel about her?"

Naomi was annoyed by the tone of excitement in her grandmother's voice. "Yeah—well—he's just the neighbour," Naomi replied, trying to be evasive. She didn't mention their date the night before, and quickly changed the subject by telling more about her Beijing holiday. But, now, reliving that wonderful holiday for Baba and Gigi didn't seem to cheer Naomi up. After 15 minutes, Naomi made an excuse that she needed to get back to her homework, and said goodbye.

"Okay, dear. Thanks for calling us. Let me know how things go with your mother and that neighbour," said Baba as she hung up.

Naomi could tell that her grandmother had been smiling at the other end of the line, and Gigi had also sounded eager to know about this mysterious neighbour. Naomi sat on the sofa for a long time, staring at the phone in her hand. She then turned to the window and stared out at Hong Kong. A thought entered her mind: *I need someone. I need someone to need me.* Naomi got off the sofa, grabbed her backpack and was out the door.

Naomi got off the bus in Mid-levels and headed in the direction of Mother's Love. She tried to clear her mind of a growing anxiety by window-shopping along the way, but it wasn't working. Then Naomi remembered what Chen had told her about breathing exercises one day, and how they could help ease stress. Naomi tried concentrating on her breathing as she walked, taking long steady breaths and slow exhalations, hearing her own breathing in her ears. Chen's trick began to work, and Naomi felt herself calming down. The jumble of feelings; fear, anger, betrayal, loneliness, were subsiding. She focused her thoughts on a room full of laughing, playful children, that would soon be clamouring for her attention. By the time Naomi reached Mother's Love, she was smiling with anticipation.

Naomi signed in at the volunteer's register and made her way to the room at the end of the hall on the second floor. This was where the walking and crawling toddlers spent much of their play time. Naomi smiled as she opened the door a crack. She liked to peek inside the room at first, to see if any of the children would notice her. Someone always did, so eager were they to play. Naomi loved their excited cries as they rushed to the door. Naomi would quickly step in and close the door behind her before they got too close, and then drop to the floor and let them fall all over her with big hugs and kisses. Sometimes there would be another volunteer in the room, enjoying the interaction as much as Naomi, but, more often, there was only the house assistant to care for the children.

On this day, Naomi peeked in the door and saw a girl sitting on the floor among the group of boisterous children and their assortment of toys. *She looks about my age,* Naomi thought. *Another volunteer?* The girl looked up briefly at Naomi, then watched in surprise as the children turned to follow her gaze and move en masse towards Naomi.

"Hi, I'm Naomi," Naomi said to the girl, then began to laugh as she reached to hug two little girls and a boy all at once. Instantly, Naomi felt cheerful. The feelings she'd been grappling with on her way over were forgotten, and she reached to scoop up another little girl who'd managed to crawl into her lap. *They need me,* she thought happily. It felt good to be needed. Naomi turned to the girl after a few moments, realizing that she had heard no response to her greeting.

"Is this your first visit as a volunteer?" Naomi asked cheerfully. She thought she noticed something in the girl's face. The young woman looked at Naomi, then down at the child in her lap. *Oops. Maybe she doesn't speak English,* Naomi thought. Naomi mumbled an apology, realizing her error.

The young woman raised her eyes to Naomi's. "I'm staying here."

Naomi's eyes opened wide and they darted to the girl's abdomen, before she realized that her shocked reaction was quickly becoming obvious. Naomi could barely discern the bulge under the girl's baggy sweater, but there definitely was one. Quickly Naomi returned her gaze to the girl's face, as she felt her own becoming warm with embarrassment.

The young woman was not a volunteer. *You're pregnant?* Naomi almost blurted out. *But you can't be any older than me!*

The girl knew exactly what Naomi was thinking. She smiled wanly as she put a hand over her stomach.

Naomi smiled back, not sure what to say. Desperate to deflect the issue, she hugged one of the children again and started making clown faces at the others around her, bringing on a round of giggles and laughter. Naomi laughed back at them, but was feeling increasingly uncomfortable. Through the corner of her eye, Naomi could see the girl staring at her as she played with the children.

"You're good with the children," the girl said after a time. "I don't know what to do."

"It's easy. They're all great—" Naomi replied, trying to sound relaxed. She didn't look at the girl when she spoke.

"I come here—to play with the children—because I don't have anything else to do, while I am here," the girl said. Naomi turned to watch the girl pull at her sweater, trying to hide her slightly rounded belly. It looked to Naomi as if the girl was going to cry.

"What's your name?" Naomi asked, not knowing what else to say, but feeling that she had to say something—anything at all.

"Grace," the girl replied in a small voice.

Neither girl spoke for several minutes. Only the sound of children playing and laughing could be heard. The door opened, and the assistant walked in. She looked over from the young girl to Naomi, and smiled. "Have you two introduced yourselves? Grace, this is Naomi—one of our star volunteers." She beamed at Naomi, and gestured towards the pregnant girl, smiling. "And this is Grace. She's a new resident. Our only resident, in fact, at the moment." The assistant looked at Naomi intently for several seconds, then spoke. "It will be bath time for the children soon." She paused again, "Grace, would you like your dinner in the sitting room upstairs instead of your own room? Maybe Naomi would like to join you—if you want some company." Naomi looked at the assistant in surprise. The woman quickly added with a smile, "If you stay, Naomi, I promise to let you help put the children to bed."

Naomi laughed with joy, momentarily forgetting her discomfort. She had never had the chance to put the children to bed, although she had heard once from another volunteer that it was a lot of fun cuddling and rocking to sleep all the snugly, freshly-washed youngsters. "You bet," she replied.

Grace smiled shyly, "I don't mind."

The assistant smiled warmly at Grace. "Fine. You take Naomi upstairs and I'll have someone bring up your trays in a few minutes."

The assistant rounded up the children and Grace lead Naomi upstairs to the sitting room on the residents' floor. They sat down on the sofa and Grace reached for the television's remote control. Naomi looked around the little room. A small vase of plastic flowers stood alone on the mantel over an artificial fireplace. The flower-print curtains hung limply. Naomi thought the room looked a little dreary.

"I don't think this room is used very much," said Grace. "But I haven't been here very long." Naomi watched Grace as she played absently with the remote control. And then Grace said, "They're not going to come to see me—Mom said." Her head was bowed, and the remote control was now clutched tightly in her hand.

"Here you are. Dinner," announced one of the kitchen staff as she entered the room and placed a large tray on the coffee table in front of the two girls. Grace and Naomi leaned over to see what was being offered: a chicken stir-fry and, of course, rice, with a plate of pineapple slices for dessert. Naomi watched Grace reach for her plate eagerly. The girl looked up at Naomi and grinned as she brought a forkful to her mouth.

"I do get hungry—these days," she said with a little grin.

Naomi took a bite herself and was pleasantly surprised. "The food is good here."

"It's okay," Grace said. The two ate in silence for several minutes.

"I'm glad I found out about this place," said Grace. "It's better than living in the street."

Naomi looked up sharply at Grace. Barely believing what this girl was saying to her, Naomi started to eat more quickly. Chewing her food was a way to prevent herself from asking the questions that were ricocheting around in her mind: *What happened? Of course you know what happened, Naomi, stupid, she's pregnant. How pregnant are you? How come you're here? Where is your family? Do they know where you are? Do you feel alone? Are you okay? Are you excited? Are you afraid? Are you going to keep the baby? What are going to do?*

Grace looked over at Naomi. It was clear to the girl that her new dinner partner—a stranger named Naomi—had questions. She said quietly, "I'm almost five months pregnant now."

Naomi gulped down a mouthful of rice. "Oh, I see. Well, you don't look it," Naomi offered. *That was a stupid thing to say! I have no idea what she's supposed to look like,* Naomi berated herself.

Grace smiled. "My tummy is starting to show. That's why I decided to come here now." After a few more bites, she asked, "What made you come here? You're a volunteer, right?"

Naomi nodded. She thought about telling Grace about the girl she had seen at the bus station in Guangzhou, and how it had got her mother thinking about volunteering at Mother's Love, but decided against it. "Oh, I like coming here to play with the kids. My mom started coming here first, when we had just moved here. We're from Canada. I decided to come, too, you know, just to try something different. I never thought I'd end up volunteering at—a place like this, when I first came to Hong Kong." Naomi smiled, picturing the rosy-cheeked faces of her little charges, and continued, "I really like coming here. I usually come on weekends but—" Naomi's eyes darkened as she thought about her phone call with Baba that day, "I just felt like coming today."

Grace asked Naomi questions about her life in Hong Kong, and Naomi told Grace about practising *tai chi* in the park with Chen. Then Naomi began to talk about her friends and school and realized that Grace's face was becoming clouded with sadness. Naomi realized she had said the wrong thing. *Could she be a student—like me? Naomi wondered. If she is, then she's left her friends behind. I wonder how she'll ever be able to face them all again.*

Grace wasn't going to share her feelings. The girl reached for her paper napkin and began to wipe tears from her eyes. Naomi sat silent and still, again not knowing what to do, as the girl cried next to her on the sofa. After a few moments, Naomi put her plate on the coffee table and slid over to the weeping girl. A bit awkwardly, Naomi reached to put an arm over Grace's hunched shoulders. "I'm sorry. I shouldn't have started talking about school—"

"It's okay. I'm okay. I'm sorry," replied Grace, as she stared down at the plate in her lap. "I'm happy to talk to you. It's nice to have someone to talk to." She looked up at Naomi. "It was nice meeting you, Naomi."

"Nice meeting you, too, Grace," Naomi replied with a little smile.

Grace wiped her eyes again before returning her attention to her dinner, and the two girls finished their meal in silence. Naomi looked out the window, and was surprised to see that it was already dark.

"I should be going. My mother's going to wonder where I am," Naomi said, then regretted uttering those words. *I know nothing about this girl. Maybe she's a runaway, and maybe there are people wondering where she is, too. Or maybe her parents have kicked her out of the house—and nobody cares.* "I'm going to go now." Naomi said, and stood up slowly.

"But what about the children's bedtime?" Grace asked.

Naomi had forgotten. "Next time," she replied, forcing a smile.

Grace nodded and looked at Naomi hopefully. "Will I see you again soon?"

"I usually come on Saturdays," Naomi replied as she backed out of the room. After signing out and saying goodbye to the desk staff, Naomi headed out the door into a bracing January wind. She buttoned up her coat, having decided to walk home instead of catching a bus. Naomi wanted some time to think about things—it seemed to her that life was becoming more and more complicated.

Kung Hei Fat Choi! Welcome to the Year of the Monkey! This year will be fast-paced and full of surprises, just like the clever, restless Monkey. And although it can at times be very cunning, the Monkey's sociable nature means it never wishes harm to others. Still, as surprises can bring both good and bad fortune, the Year of the Monkey may be a difficult time for those who cannot learn to accept the Monkey's unpredictable nature.

—Hong Kong Tourist Authority

"I'm not going with you," Naomi announced, and braced herself for her mother's reaction.

"What are you talking about? Of course you're going," Sara countered. Her voice registered bewilderment more than anything else. "You told Steve you'd come."

"That was ages ago! He didn't even give me a chance to make my own plans!" Naomi shot back. "I'm going to spend the day with Jovita and her family. She's going to take me to see lions dancing, or something like that. Dinner with her family." Naomi was relieved to have a good excuse to break her promise—an invitation from her best friend—but the truth was, she didn't want to go out on a date with her mother and Steve. She wished Steve had never asked them in the first place.

Sara looked at her daughter for a long time. "Well, I suppose that would be more interesting for you, anyway. But I wish you would have said something sooner. It's a matter of being polite—"

"Sorry," Naomi mumbled. She didn't want to hear anything more about it. "I've got to get ready."

"Wait."

Naomi turned around, shoulders tensed, ready for another confrontation.

"We'll pick you up after dinner at Jovita's place and go to the fireworks together," Sara said.

The expression on her mother's face told Naomi that she would be asking for trouble if she argued. Naomi fixed a nasty stare on her mother before storming off.

"Hey, Jovita!" Naomi called out as she jogged up to her friend, who was waiting at the bus stop. "Lead the way—far away from here!"

Jovita shot Naomi a surprised look.

"I'd rather be spending the day with you than Mom and Steve," Naomi said by way of explanation.

Jovita was well aware of her friend's anxiety over the subject of her neighbour, and had no desire to make light of the situation. But even so, Jovita felt compelled to ask, "Still, Naomi? What's wrong? Is he really that weird?"

Naomi grimaced and shook her head. "No—he's normal, I suppose. I just don't want him around. Mom and I are fine by ourselves. He—confuses things." She looked at Jovita and continued, "Anyway, he's taking her out on a junk for the day. And I told Mom I didn't want to go. But she said I—we—have to go to the fireworks with them later on—"

"Junk trip? Lucky!" Jovita crooned as a bus pulled up.

Naomi whispered hoarsely into her friend's ear as they took their seats. "But I like things the way they are. What if he dates Mom and then they split up? Mom would be really upset about it." Naomi couldn't even put words to the possibility of something more substantial happening. Memories of her parents' divorce loomed large in Naomi's mind. And then her father's remarriage—and the little boy. She shook her head. "We don't need him—Steve," Naomi said.

Jovita looked over at her friend with concern, and put a reassuring hand on Naomi's shoulder. "You seem real steamed. Have you talked to your mom about how you feel?"

"No. Well, a little—kind of. But, you know, it doesn't really seem like a big deal to her," Naomi replied, waving her hand. "She says he's just a nice guy—a helpful neighbour. And that we're lucky."

Jovita nodded sympathetically.

The bus took the girls to Victoria Park, where one of the many Chinese New Year's festivals held across Hong Kong was in full swing. The park was overflowing with eager spectators dressed for the winter chill. Although there was no snow, the temperature had dropped to freezing in recent nights. Naomi surveyed the crowd; red was a clear favourite for clothing on this day. Naomi noticed that children especially were dressed up, and most were holding a toy or candy as they strolled with their parents and grandparents among the stalls that lined the pathways in the park. In one section, vendors sold a variety of cut flowers, in addition to the pussy willows and long branches of pink peach blossoms which were especially popular for the occasion. Naomi noticed that flower bulbs, in particular those of the paperwhite, and miniature orange trees were also selling briskly. Naomi stood back, admiring the riot of colour and the festive air, and snapped a photo of Jovita standing among the blossoms. "It's strange to see all these flowers at a New Year's festival," Naomi said. "Where I come from, it's all just snow—and more snow."

"Chinese New Year is also called Spring Festival here," Jovita said. "I especially love looking at all the flowers. But the food is good, too."

Jovita led Naomi to a row of food stalls; the smells of fried noodles, grilled meats, and curries filled the air. She pointed to a table laden with bamboo trays, from which clouds of steam were rising. "Over there, Naomi," Jovita said, "is my favourite—*jiaozi*—a meat dumpling. It means 'sleep together and have sons'. Having sons is very important in Chinese culture." Naomi nodded and sniffed the air. The warm, savoury aroma was tempting, but Naomi turned away. She wasn't hungry.

Farther along, Naomi and Jovita came across a table piled high with exquisitely wrapped boxes. On the table in front, open giftboxes revealed several compartments, each filled with various sweets: sugared fruits, nuts, and a sesame seed and honey concoction that Naomi thought looked scrumptious. "The food has symbolic meaning," Jovita said, pointing to a mound of gold crescent-shaped delicacies. "This is *yau gwok*—its shape is supposed to resemble a gold ingot." Jovita turned to Naomi and grinned. "As you know, at Chinese New Year, the thing we wish for the most is prosperity. And, as you can see, we eat a lot of this at Chinese New Year."

Naomi smiled, and thought she could detect a drum beat in the distance.

"The lion is coming!" Jovita cried out. She grabbed Naomi's arm and led her towards the centre of the park. Naomi could hear the drumbeat and the clashing of cymbals becoming louder. Naomi gaped in awe when she finally saw the source of the din; an enormous red and green lion was dancing in the centre of the crowd, propelled by the beat. Naomi watched the lion dance, completely entranced. The great lion's body was at least 15 metres in length. It writhed and contorted its body to the rhythmic beat, jutting its head in and out towards the crowd. Naomi could see that the mouth and the eyelids of the great beast were also flapping up and down, cleverly controlled by the dancer beneath. There were more than a dozen people under the lion costume, strutting and jumping. The finale of the lion dance came when the beast climbed onto a series of poles that rose above the crowd. It was a remarkable feat of balance and athletic ability for the dancers, and the crowd applauded its admiration. Finally, when the great lion stood atop the highest pole, it released a scroll. The scroll unfurled to the ground, revealing a message in Chinese wishing everyone a happy new year. The dancers lifted off their lion costume and bowed to the appreciative audience.

"Awesome," said Naomi, applauding vigorously.

Later, Naomi bought a box of candies for Jovita's family, and then the two girls headed back to Jovita's place for dinner. When they arrived, Naomi was greeted by a room full of strangers. Jovita's three grandparents, an aunt and an uncle, and two younger cousins were talking animatedly with Jovita's mother, father and brother. Jovita made quick introductions in Cantonese and then looked mischievously at her friend. "I'm going to change before we see the fireworks. Practise your Cantonese, Naomi. We don't always speak English in Hong Kong." She scampered to her bedroom and shut the door, leaving Naomi alone with Jovita's exuberant extended family. Jovita's brother gave Naomi a juice and Naomi found herself seated on the floor between two giggling girls who plied her with questions about snowy Canadian winters.

Mr. Wu, Jovita's father, broke into the conversation. "Don't monopolize our guest, girls," he said with mock seriousness before asking Naomi, "Have you enjoyed the famous lion dance? I know Jovita's looking forward to the fireworks tonight—that has always been her favourite part." He paused, then thrust his chin in the direction of Jovita's bedroom. "She's got some new clothes especially for the Chinese New Year." He smiled and shook his head. "You girls, always interested in dressing up. Clothes—and boys—"

"Just clothes—for now anyway—Dad," Jovita shot back as she entered the room. Giggling, Naomi turned and looked with admiration at her friend. Jovita walked to the middle of the room and pirouetted. "Well? What do you think?" she asked. Jovita was wearing a crimson silk jacket with wide gold cuffs, and matching wool trousers. The jacket had a mandarin collar and was fastened in front by a row of Chinese-style toggles. The black boots set off the outfit beautifully, and matched her sleek black hair.

"I think I'm looking positively shabby," Naomi replied, looking down at her own rather casual outfit of blue jeans and gray-blue turtleneck sweater under a brown leather jacket.

"Hardly! You're very chic—casually elegant—as always," Jovita replied, and then added. "Actually, I'm doing this for you, you know, Naomi."

"What do you mean?" asked Naomi.

"This is a traditional thing," Jovita said, straightening out her arms for Naomi to see the jacket more easily. "Well, the jacket is, anyway—"

Her father cut in, "Well, if you want to show off traditional Chinese dress, why don't you put on your lovely red *cheongsam* I love so much—"

Jovita looked at her father in mock horror. "A dress? Dad! It's freezing out there!"

"I think you look lovely, Jovita," said Mrs. Wu, who was setting down a tray on the coffee table. "The jacket is lovely, and the colours—red and gold—look wonderful on you." She turned to Naomi and explained, "In China, red symbolizes good luck, long life and happiness. Gold, of course, represents wealth and prosperity. This is what we wish for at Chinese New Year." Then Mrs. Wu reached into her pocket and handed Naomi a small red envelope embossed with gold Chinese writing. "*Kung Hei Fat Choi*, Naomi. Happy Chinese New Year."

"Thank you, Mrs. Wu," Naomi replied as she accepted the strange offering.

"It's called *lai see*," one of Jovita's cousins explained, and grinned. "It's money!"

Naomi began to shake her head, declining the gift. She looked at Mrs. Wu, who looked at her with twinkling eyes.

"Relax, Naomi. It's not much money," Jovita said with a mixture of mirth and impatience. "Just a token. Older people always give young people money at Chinese New Year. It's a Chinese custom."

When the doorbell rang later in the evening, everyone was just finishing dinner. Naomi looked at her watch and was surprised at how the time had raced by around the crowded dinner table. Naomi had enjoyed the family banter, and thought about how her own family gatherings were so much smaller and quieter. Naomi watched Jovita run to the door, and at that moment she realized the real reason why her friend had decided to dress up for the evening. "Hello there, Naomi's mother—and you must be Steve—" Naomi heard Jovita say as she led Sara and Steve into the living room.

Mr. Wu got up from the table and crossed the room to shake hands. "*Kung Hei Fat Choi*," he said with a welcoming smile.

"Hello there. We're so happy to finally meet Naomi's parents—" Mrs. Wu began.

Sara and Steve laughed. Jovita winced. Throats were being cleared.

"He's not my father," Naomi said quietly.

"I guess—I spoke too soon," Mrs. Wu said with an embarrassed laugh.

Steve's deep laughter filled the room. "No, I'm not as lucky to have a daughter as lovely as these two here," he said, gesturing towards Naomi and Jovita. Naomi rolled her eyes and caught sight of Jovita, who was looking at Steve with shining eyes. Naomi watched Jovita flick her hair behind one shoulder, and shook her head.

Steve winked at Naomi as he reached to shake Mr. and Mrs. Wu's hands. "I'm Steve—Naomi's neighbour. Nice to finally meet you, too."

"Have a great time down with the crowds tonight," said Mr. Wu. "My wife and I are content to watch the fireworks from the comfort of home this year."

Sara laughed, "Well, this is something new for us, and we wouldn't want to miss it. It was lovely to meet you and your big family. And thank you for having Naomi over for dinner," Sara said before the four stepped out the door.

As Sara and Steve walked on ahead towards the waterside several blocks away, Jovita grabbed Naomi's arm and whispered into her friend's ear, "He's gorgeous, Naomi. I wonder what his sign is—"

"He's a Tiger—I checked," Naomi replied, avoiding Jovita's gaze.

"Ah, he's a Tiger! Fearless and protective. Powerful, passionate and a bit of a rebel—"

"Enough—" Naomi cut in.

"Oh, but Naomi, it's perfect—"

"Stop!" Naomi hissed.

The look on Naomi's face told Jovita it was time to stop teasing, and sadness clouded her twinkling eyes. "Naomi," Jovita began. The girl wasn't sure if it was any of her business, but it was clear that her friend was hurting. "I'm sorry," was all Jovita could say.

Naomi, Jovita, Sara, and Steve joined the crowds congregating at the harbour front and gazed in wonder at the Hong Kong skyline. Many of the largest skyscrapers had been decorated with impressive coloured lights which were lit up in an assortment of seasonal motifs. Naomi was admiring the lights when Steve walked up beside her.

"It's a nice night for the fireworks. We're lucky. It can be pretty overcast at this time of year. And it's not so cold tonight, either," Steve said.

Naomi nodded.

There was an awkward silence. "How are you finding Hong Kong, then, Naomi?"

A slight smile spread across Naomi's lips, and she nodded again. "I am really enjoying it. It's so interesting."

"I think so, too," Steve said. More silence.

"Almost time for the fireworks!" Jovita shouted above the noise. At that moment, a high pitched whooshing sound pierced the air, followed by a loud pop. Everyone looked up to the sky as a burst of white and red and yellow exploded in the darkness. More colours followed, and after 15 minutes the fireworks reached a breathtaking multi-coloured crescendo before stopping abruptly, leaving only a trail of smoke and the memories of sound and light.

"Wasn't that great?" Steve said. Before Naomi knew it, Steve had bent down and kissed her gently on the cheek. "Happy New Year, Naomi," he said. He turned to Jovita with a smile, "Happy New Year, Jovita."

Naomi watched as Steve turned to give her mother an equally chaste kiss on the cheek. "Happy New Year, Sara."

"You, too, Steve," Sara responded. Naomi's eyes darkened. Her mother's eyes seemed a little too bright, her face a little too cheerful. Naomi listened to her mother and Steve chatter as they walked all the way back to Happy Valley, aware of the unmistakable lilt in her mother's voice.

The Dragon is the highest celestial power, and a born traveller, always seeking out exotic adventures. The strong and independent Dragon often prefers solitude, though others will be drawn to its charisma. Energetic and filial, the Dragon is admired by all even though it can at times be quick-tempered, impetuous and stubborn. The Dragon girl has fine self-worth, sometimes to the point of over-confidence. When she does make mistakes like the rest of us, she may not believe it! However, once the Dragon sees the error of her ways (this may take some time), she will endeavour tenaciously to set things right.

Famous Dragons: Sigmund Freud, Joan of Arc
—Star Signs, Love Signs, by the Mystical Madame Li

The following Saturday morning Naomi jumped out of bed at 6:30, eager to be out of the house and getting on with things. Naomi looked at the phone as she entered the kitchen, and decided she wasn't going to call Jovita to see what she was doing. *She's probably going to do some kind of family holiday thing,* Naomi told herself, but then admitted that she just needed a little time away from her friend. *I'm not happy with you,* Naomi thought, as she eyed the telephone. Naomi remembered how Jovita had rushed to the door to greet her mother and Steve on the night of the fireworks, and decided that her friend's friendly attitude towards

Steve was a betrayal of sorts. Naomi's thoughts shifted to the walk home after the fireworks, and her mother's excited, almost giggly, voice as she talked with Steve. Naomi shrugged as she poured herself some tea, hoping to rid herself of the negativity that seemed to be draped like a weight around her shoulders. Naomi felt she needed this day to occupy herself with her own pursuits, and was particularly looking forward to her *tai chi* lesson with Chen. Naomi knew that part of what she was feeling was about avoiding Steve, and anyone who had anything to do with him. *That's about everyone I know these days—even Baba and Gigi,* Naomi thought sadly as she took her mug of tea and sat by the window to gaze out at Hong Kong. She felt very alone.

Naomi waved eagerly to Chen as she jogged into the park, and realized that the old man was by himself this morning. "Private lesson today," Chen chuckled, noticing Naomi's quizzical look. "I've given everyone the day off, because of Chinese New Year."

Naomi smiled and nodded, and instantly felt more light-hearted. The sight of Chen's familiar, cheerful face filled her with gratitude. She understood that the others were probably visiting their sons and daughters and grandchildren today. Suddenly Naomi wondered why Chen was in the park at all. "Don't you have any family to see over the holidays?" she asked.

Chen smiled at Naomi and shook his head. There was a silence, and then Chen said simply, "I have a brother in China. He lives in Guanxi province, where we were born. He's got a wife, a grown son, and a granddaughter now. I haven't seen them in a long time, but we keep in touch." Chen clapped his hands. "All right, Naomi. Let's push our boat with the current, shall we?"

"Good idea," Naomi answered. They took their positions and, at Chen's signal, began the routine. 'Pushing the boat with the current' was one of the first *tai chi* manoeuvres Naomi had learned. As she followed Chen's movements, Naomi thought about what she had been learning during these lessons with the old man. Naomi loved the way *tai chi* routines had names, such as 'Five cloud hands', 'Step up to seven stars', and 'Embrace tiger, return to mountain'. Sometimes, after the lesson, Chen would spend a few minutes sitting on the bench with Naomi to talk about the contemplative nature of *tai chi*. He explained in detail about the

Chinese philosophy, called *Taoism,* from which *tai chi* developed. The more Naomi practised, the more she understood how the Taoist principles of centredness, balance, yielding, and rootedness, as well as an appreciation of nature, were reflected in what she was doing. Naomi loved her *tai chi* practise, and had never missed a lesson with Chen from the day she started almost five months earlier. Practising *tai chi* always made Naomi feel calm inside and good about herself and, today especially, she was grateful for that feeling.

"Very good, Naomi," Chen said. His eyes smiled his approval. "You are improving."

"I've got a good teacher," Naomi replied with a grin.

Chen chuckled and waved off the compliment. "I cannot teach you. I can only show you," he replied, then added with a grin. "And then I never worry that you will be able to figure it out for yourself."

Naomi smiled back at him. "Well, thank you for the confidence, Chen. But I still think you're a good teacher—the best."

Chen laughed. "Okay, okay. White crane spreads wings," he announced. He and Naomi began a new series of moves. After several more minutes of practise, Chen decided the lesson was over. He walked over to the bench, opened his backpack, and handed Naomi a small red envelope, similar to the one she had received from Jovita's mother. "*Kung Hei Fat Choi.*"

"Thank you very much, Chen. *Kung Hei Fat Choi* to you, too." Naomi accepted the red envelope with a bow.

As they sat down on the bench, Chen turned and asked. "How have you spent the holidays, Naomi?"

"I visited my friend Jovita and her big family. I was given a *lai see* there, too," Naomi replied, holding up the envelope Chen had just given her. "A very lucrative custom." She and Chen chuckled. "I saw the lion dance, too—awesome! And we went to the flower festival in the park—so beautiful. The park was packed!" Naomi stopped to catch her breath, and it was a few moments before she continued. "In the evening, Jovita and I walked down to the harbour to watch the fireworks. We went with my mom—and my neighbour." Naomi added after a thought, "His name is Steve." She looked down at her running shoes and continued. "I think he likes my mom—she's divorced."

Chen looked over at Naomi and nodded. After several moments, he asked, "Does your mother like Steve?"

"I think—she likes him, too," Naomi replied. She watched her heel make lines in the dirt.

"And you?"

Naomi looked up, then down at her shoe again and shook her head. "He's a nice guy. But I don't know if I want him to date my mom—"

"Why not, Naomi?" Chen asked gently.

Naomi didn't look up. "If they did, then they broke up, Mom would be hurt."

Chen nodded thoughtfully, then put his hand gently on Naomi's shoulder. "Do you think that is the only reason why you don't want your mother to see this man?"

Naomi's breath caught. She looked at up Chen and shrugged sullenly.

Chen patted Naomi's shoulder, then put his hands on his knees. "Naomi, are you going to Mother's Love this morning?"

Naomi looked up, and forced a smile. "Yes. By the time Saturday rolls around, I'm really missing everyone."

"Wonderful. I'll tell you what; it'll be a slow day today at the shop. Why don't you come over after your visit there. I want to show you something."

"Okay," Naomi replied. They rose from the bench, and Naomi waited as Chen walked over to the edge of the park, to the drainage ditch. He smiled as he returned to the bench. "Just checking. No little boys playing about today."

Several hours later, Naomi opened the door to Chen's antique shop on Hollywood Road, still in high spirits from her visit with the children at Mother's Love. Naomi looked around at the familiar shop and smiled. *It even smells familiar,* Naomi thought. *Dust, old book and things, incense, maybe tea.* She looked at the Buddha statue and the old photographs that were propped up on the shelf at the back of the shop. Naomi watched minute trails of smoke rise languidly towards the ceiling from the incense sticks placed in front of the photos. At that moment, the curtain was drawn back, and Chen appeared with a welcoming smile. Naomi was aware of a 'clack-clack' sound coming from the back room.

"Welcome Naomi. How are the children—and your friend Grace—doing today?" he asked.

"Oh, they're wonderful, Chen!" Naomi beamed. "And they're especially excited about the Chinese New Year. Apparently a big lion visited and danced for them in the courtyard." Naomi added wistfully, "I wish I could have seen those kids' faces." Her wistful expression turned to a frown and she asked, "What's that sound, Chen?"

Chen smiled, "My friends are here, playing *mahjong*. Come see." He pulled back the curtain and waved Naomi in. Two women and two men, whom Naomi recognized from her *tai chi* group, were seated around a card table, deeply engrossed in the game. On the table were many small, white, rectangular tiles with blue, green and red symbols printed on them. They were taking turns reaching for tiles and shuffling them together in long lines, which produced the distinctive clacking noise Naomi was hearing. They looked up at Naomi and smiled only briefly, continuing to play the game with single-minded concentration. It was clear to Naomi that *mahjong* was serious business. Chen looked at his friends, put his hands on his hips, and chuckled. "They may be here all day. *Mahjong* is a very popular game. I believe it's similar to a card game called Gin Rummy." Naomi nodded, and Chen added with a wink, "I don't play much myself. I have to keep an eye on the shop."

Naomi followed Chen back into the shop. A customer was browsing and Chen approached the woman to offer assistance. Naomi occupied herself by looking around at all the wonderful things in the shop. She was always intrigued by Chen's eclectic assortment; expensive-looking vases, old Chinese scroll paintings and dusty furniture, as well as ceramic ornaments of all kinds. Once again Naomi found herself looking in wonder at Chen's large collection of Chairman Mao memorabilia from the Chinese mainland. She was fascinated by the assortment of pins, posters, little red books, and ceramic busts, every one of them carrying Mao Zedong's image.

Chen returned to Naomi as the customer exited the shop. He picked up a little shiny red book of Chairman Mao's quotations, and chuckled. "These are very popular with tourists," he said. "I think you would call them 'hot-sellers'."

Naomi nodded. "Where did all these little books come from?" she asked.

Chen's eyes darkened a little. He put the book down gently on the table and said in an even tone, "Years ago, in China, everyone had such a book. It was important to have one—in fact, it was compulsory." Chen turned to Naomi, "There was a time—in English, it was called the Cultural Revolution—"

Naomi cut in. "Oh, yes, Mom's friend told me about it. She said it was a difficult time for everyone. She called it a 'madness'."

Chen nodded, and Naomi thought she saw a glint of sadness in his eyes. "Yes, it was a madness, indeed. Society in China at that time was in a state of upheaval. Most Chinese families have been affected by it, in one way or another." He surveyed the assortment of Chairman Mao items and said slowly, "It's true—these are good for business. But I sometimes think the real reason I have them here is to help me—come to terms, as you say—with the past."

Naomi studied Chen's face, which had seemed to age right before her eyes. Naomi wanted to know if there was a part of Chen's past that was troubling him, but she dared not ask. Then, with a little smile and a shrug, Chen motioned Naomi over to the counter at the back of the room. "I have a little something for you," he said.

Naomi took a seat on a bench behind the counter as Chen went into the back room, and soon emerged with the small, worn book she had seen earlier. "Do you remember, Naomi, our conversions about Chinese philosophy?"

Naomi nodded. "Yes. Like Confucius—and Taoism. Different ways of thinking about ourselves and our destiny," Naomi replied.

"That's right," Chen said. "*Tai chi* is an aspect of Taoism—one particular philosophy—or way of thinking. In fact, I learned how to speak English by reading this philosophy, in this book called the *Tao Te Ching*."

Naomi eyed the slim volume in Chen's hand. "You learned English by reading that book?" Naomi asked. "That can't be the easiest way to learn a foreign language."

Chen chuckled. "Well, I knew a little English before then, but it wasn't very good. When I came to Hong Kong—" all at once Chen stopped talking. Naomi looked up. Chen's eyes had become very bright.

"I knew I had better improve my English, so I decided to do it through my studies of this ancient Chinese text." He grinned, "And I am still studying it!"

"Wow!" Naomi replied. "Then I'm sure I'll never figure it out."

"Don't worry, Naomi," Chen replied, "Like all philosophies, you may agree with it, or you may not. It has helped me." He riffled the pages. "Some people think the *Tao Te Ching* is also a way to better understand how Chinese people think," Chen added. His eyes were smiling. "For example, the *Tao* says, 'yield and overcome'. Can you understand how it applies to *tai chi*?"

Naomi pondered this for a moment, and nodded.

"Perhaps, in English, a similar expression would be to 'go with the flow'."

Naomi smiled, and nodded. *It's true*, she thought, intrigued.

Chen smiled. "Think about this idea next time something—or someone—new comes into your life."

All of a sudden, Naomi's mind clouded over. *He's talking to me about Steve*, Naomi thought, a little indignantly. She shook her head at Chen. "I know. That sounds—fine. But life's not so simple, Chen. Why can't things just stay the way they are. We have another saying in English: If it ain't broke, don't fix it." Naomi clenched her fists and looked straight ahead. "We don't need him." Naomi put her hand over her mouth. She looked up at Chen and smiled wanly. Her little outburst about Steve had caught her off guard. "I can be pretty stubborn, I admit," she said. "After all, I'm a Dragon—stubborn, egotistical. Independent and a bit of a loner. But I'm proud of it!"

"Ah, so you know all about Chinese horoscopes—your animal sign." Chen said. He looked at Naomi for a long while and scratched his head. "Our sign can really tell us a lot about who we are. Only if we know who we are, can we really begin to understand what we need in our lives." Chen continued, "And, in this way, we can begin to discover our true destiny." He looked at Naomi for a few more moments. "So, you think you are all those things, Naomi? Independent? A loner? Egotistical? I must admit, I don't see that." He laughed and shook his head, then looked at Naomi with a puzzled expression. "Are you sure you're a Dragon?"

Naomi threw her head back in surprise and laughed. "Of course I'm sure. I'm a Dragon all right. I've known I was a dragon ever since I first heard about Chinese horoscopes—they use them in Japan too, you know. Yes, I'm a Dragon." She smiled at Chen. "In fact, my birthday is just next week—"

"Really? When exactly is your birthday?" Chen asked. There was a hint of a smile on his lips.

"February third," Naomi replied happily. "I'll be sixteen—"

Chen began to laugh. He looked at Naomi with twinkling eyes. "It is just as I thought, Naomi. I am afraid to tell you this—but you are not a Dragon!" He shook his head and chuckled some more.

"What do you mean I'm not a Dragon. I *am* a Dragon!" Naomi shot back in surprise and dismay. "I read it in a book when I lived in Japan—" Naomi paused, then blurted out, "—I—I *want* to be a Dragon!"

Chen put a hand on Naomi's shoulder. "It's true that the year you were born is referred to as the Year of the Dragon. And perhaps, in Japan, they use the calendar year—in other words, from January 1 to December 31—to calculate one's animal sign. But you must understand, Naomi, the Chinese calendar is a *lunar* calendar. And the Chinese New Year is a *lunar* new year—" Chen laughed some more. "That means it changes with the cycle of the moon. Did you not realize that, Naomi?"

Naomi shook her head, not quite sure where Chen was heading.

Chen pointed to an old book on the shelf next to the small Buddha statue. "Could you get me that book, Naomi. I shall prove it to you."

Naomi placed the dusty book in Chen's hands and he flipped through the book to a chart. Naomi watched Chen's finger scroll down to the year of Naomi's birth. She followed Chen's finger across the page. *Dragon: February 17, 1988 to February 5, 1989.*

"It's true, Chinese New Year came a little early this year—*before* your birthday. But, in 1988, the Dragon year commenced *after* your birthday. You, Naomi, are a Rabbit!" Chen watched with amusement as Naomi's face registered the news. He smiled warmly at the surprised young girl, whom he had grown to care for in the last few months. "But, I must say, Naomi—as a Rabbit born so close to the Year of the Dragon, you do have some of the Great Dragon's qualities. The very best ones."

The Rabbit is born under the signs of virtue and prudence. It does not like to be in stressful situations, for it is a cautious planner and does not like to take risks. Above all, the Rabbit likes a secure, calm, and stable environment. It craves the love and warmth of family and friends above all else.

Famous Rabbits: King Bhumibol, Jomo Kenyatta
—Star Signs Love Signs, by the Mystical Madame Li

"**N**aomi, how would you like to invite a bunch of your friends for dinner to celebrate your sweet sixteenth," Sara asked as she and Naomi headed to the bus stop.

Naomi smiled, waved to Chen and his friends in the park across the street, then turned to her mother. "I'd love it, Mom. Where do we get to go?" Naomi was glad for the opportunity to play host to her group of girlfriends.

"It's your choice," Sara replied.

"Great! We'll go to The Peak. By tram. We'll sit outside on the stone patio by the fireplace looking out over Aberdeen and Lamma Island," Naomi said eagerly. "Jovita, of course, Caroline, Ming, Mandy—"

"Wonderful. It'll be nice to finally meet all your friends in person," Sara said, then added with a playful smile, "And not have to peek at you sitting with them at lunchtime."

"Sorry, Mom," Naomi mumbled sheepishly. She knew her mother was referring to the fact that she rarely approached her at school. "It's just that—you're a teacher. My friends know it, but I don't think it's necessary that *everyone* at school know." Naomi patted her mother's back apologetically and grinned. "I know you understand."

The bus approached, and Sara gave her daughter's shoulder a playful squeeze. "Sure Naomi, I understand; you have a life. You're growing up and finding your own identity. You're not just my daughter." Sara stared intently at Naomi for a few moments, then added. "Would you mind if I asked Steve to join us? I know he'd be delighted to get an invitation from you—"

Naomi sucked in her breath, unprepared for that request but dreading it just the same. Naomi looked down at the sidewalk, wondering how to respond.

"If you don't want him to come, that's okay," Sara said after a few moments, then chuckled. "It's just that your old Mom would like some adult company while you girls talk your girl talk—"

Naomi nodded with a grimace, *I don't think Mom's being totally honest about that!* "How about May or Edith?" she asked. She looked at her mother and saw the surprised and disappointed look on her face. All at once Naomi felt ashamed. She knew she was being unfair and selfish— and not very neighbourly. "Never mind, Mom," she added hastily. "*You* can ask him."

Sara brightened, "All right, then. I will."

Naomi turned to look out the window of the bus. *Now all my friends are going to meet the guy they've been wondering about!* Naomi thought. She sighed.

At lunchtime, Naomi and her friends were, as usual, seated at a table in the cafeteria with the view over Aberdeen. "I'd like to invite you to my birthday party. It will be on Friday night at The Restaurant on The Peak. We'll take the tram up there," Naomi announced. The girls accepted eagerly.

"I love going up there," said Mandy. "The view—" she said dreamily, then added grimly, "If it's not raining."

"We'll hope for a clear, starry night. So romantic, that place—" said Caroline.

Naomi cleared her throat nervously. "You'll get to meet my neighbour," Naomi began. "Steve. That guy that has the hots for my mom."

"Is it mutual—yet?" asked Mandy with a smile on her face.

Naomi was about to reply but Jovita cut in. "I'd say so." She looked at Naomi and then around the table. "I met him at Chinese New Year. And I have to say that he's fine." Jovita glanced at Naomi again before continuing. The look on her face was almost an admonishment and she added, "In fact, I'd say he's much better than fine."

Naomi glared at Jovita and said sarcastically, "Thanks for the support."

Jovita rolled her eyes. "Look, Naomi. Your mom has a life, too." Jovita looked around at the other girls for confirmation and then turned to Naomi again. "Face it—if there was a guy here that you liked, who paid attention to you, you'd want to go out with him. Why doesn't your mom get that chance?"

Mandy added quietly, "What do you expect your mom to do, Naomi? Never date anyone ever again?"

Naomi looked down at the contents of her lunch tray. She was embarrassed that her friends had noticed her selfish attitude, and had also made an assumption about what she would do in similar circumstances. Naomi looked at her friends and chuckled, trying to make light of the situation, even though her stomach was all churned up. "Well, you guys really tell it like it is, don't you," she said quietly.

"Because we care," said Caroline. "And because it doesn't have to be as bad as you think."

"That's true—I know," added Mandy.

"Yeah, well, it's not like they're engaged, you know. You're all making it sound like it's a done deal—" Naomi shot back, surprised at how defensive she sounded.

"Nobody's saying that," Jovita cut in.

"I know," Naomi mumbled, and took a deep breath. She was out of line, and she knew it. Forcing a smile, she said, "Well, anyway, you'll all get to meet him next Friday."

Naomi and her friends were seated at the restaurant's waiting bar, as Steve and Sara stood outside on the patio waiting for their table to be called.

"Naomi, Steve and your mom are a nice-looking couple. They are obviously over the moon with each other," declared Caroline. "You really should let them date. You know—give them your stamp of approval. It's important to your mom."

"To Steve, too," Jovita added. "He's that kind of guy. A good guy. He cares about you, Naomi. He cares about what you think."

"I think they'll do what they want. It doesn't matter what I think," Naomi replied.

"Come on, Naomi. You don't think you're sending signals to your mom? Don't you think she knows how you feel?" Mandy asked. "How does that make *her* feel?"

"I know, I know," Naomi said. She held up her hands. "Just let me get used to the idea that Mom has a life—one that doesn't revolve around me." Naomi was determined not to let the conversation spoil her birthday party. And, looking over at Steve and her mother, Naomi had to admit they did look like a nice pair; relaxed and happy together. Naomi was glad she'd told her mother it was okay to bring Steve. *Yes, my mom does have a life,* she reminded herself. Naomi was eager to change the subject, and she raised her arm. "Bartender. It's my birthday. Give me a Pina Colada!" she said. Her friends giggled.

The bartender came over to Naomi and grinned. "And how old might you be?" he asked.

"Sweet sixteen," Naomi replied coquettishly.

The bartender chuckled. "Well then, I'll make it a double—and hold all the rum. How's that?"

As Naomi took a sip from her drink, Sara's name was called and everyone walked out to the table by the stone fireplace on the patio. Despite the February chill, the roaring fire created a warmth that enveloped much of the large patio. Naomi wasn't surprised to find that, at the end of the meal, several waiters and the bartender came over with a birthday cake stuck with sixteen sparklers. Soon Naomi was busy opening presents that were thrust in front of her. From Jovita, Naomi was given a fluffy pink fake-fur vest. Mandy gave her a book on *feng shui* and Ming gave her a pair of earrings. Caroline gave her a guide book about Macau, where Naomi had mentioned she and her mother would be going for the Easter holidays.

Naomi flipped through the books and surveyed her assortment of gifts. "Thank you everybody, for all the lovely gifts. And I want to tell you how much I appreciate you being my friends—"

Steve cleared his throat. "Naomi, you forgot me," he said, picking up the small box by his glass and placing it next to Naomi's plate.

Naomi stared down at the gift, feeling uncomfortable. *I hadn't forgotten your gift—I was avoiding it.*

"Just don't sit there. Open it, Naomi," Caroline urged. "Or I will."

Everyone laughed, and Naomi pulled at the ribbon on the small green box. Inside was a lovely gold rabbit pin, with a glittering pink eye. It was a stunning piece, and the girls crooned in admiration. Naomi cringed inside, knowing how Steve's choice of gift had raised him several notches in her friends' esteem. But even Naomi had to admit that the gold rabbit pin was breathtaking.

"I thought it suited you, Naomi. It's beautiful, and it's a Rabbit—like you." Steve smiled and added, "Your mother told me you used to be a Dragon, but that you are now a Rabbit. I think that's better."

Naomi looked up at her mother and Steve, sitting shoulder to shoulder at the table, framed by a string of small white lights that were strung around the patio. In that instant, Naomi saw what her girlfriends had been seeing and sensing all along; a couple who were happy together and quite possibly in love. Naomi shook the idea out of her mind, and realized that both of them were grinning at her. Jovita was giggling as she fastened the exquisite pin to Naomi's sweater, while the rest of her friends looked at each other with puzzled expressions, waiting for an explanation of Steve's strange comment.

The wise adapt themselves to circumstance, like water moulds to the pitcher.

—Chinese Proverb

"Well, Steve, I guess we better get going. The show starts at 8:00," Sara said.

From the sofa, Naomi watched them leave, cringing inside as both her mother and Steve looked over at her at the same time. *I knew they'd look at me—with that sad, 'I'm so sorry to be leaving you all alone like this' kind of look on their faces.* "Have a good time, Mom—and Steve," Naomi said, trying to sound cheerful—or at least indifferent. She thought she did a good job of it, too.

"Are you sure you're going to be okay?" Sara asked.

Naomi groaned. "How old am I?" she asked, sarcasm apparent in her tone. "I've got a video, the pizza will be arriving soon, and Jovita is on her way. What am I missing?"

Sara and Steve looked at each other and shrugged. "All right, Naomi. Have fun. We'll be home around 11:00 or so," Sara said.

"I won't wait up," Naomi said.

"Okay then. Well, goodbye, Naomi," Sara replied.

"Bye, Naomi," Steve said as he held the door open for Naomi's mother.

Naomi breathed a sigh of relief when she heard the door click shut. It was a strange kind of role reversal; being the one staying home, concerned about how the date will go and wondering what might happen. Naomi went to the kitchen and put some water in the kettle to boil. She thought about what her real concern was, and knew with a pang of guilt that she wasn't concerned about her mother's safety—as any parent would be when their child goes out on a date. *What bothers me is that Mom and Steve might discover more about each other, and like each other more.* It was a selfish though, Naomi knew, but she couldn't help it. As she stood in the kitchen waiting for the water to boil, Naomi reminded herself of the conversation she'd had with her girlfriends on her birthday. *Your mother has a life, Naomi.*

"I know. Mom has a life," Naomi said out loud as she poured some water into the teapot. She watched the water swirl and settle into the pile of tea leaves. *But Mom's life is with me.*

The doorbell rang, and Naomi could hear Jovita entering.

"Knock knock," Jovita called out.

"In here," Naomi called back from the kitchen. Naomi looked up as Jovita appeared in the doorway.

"So, they've gone on their big date?" Jovita asked with a mischievous grin.

Naomi smirked. "Acting like a couple of teenagers. Want some tea? Jasmine."

"Sure," Jovita replied, and hopped up to sit on the kitchen counter. "So what's for dinner?"

"Pepperoni and mushroom pizza," Naomi replied, pouring the tea into little cups.

Jovita's eyes grew big. "So, Naomi, where's he taking her tonight? I hope somewhere nice—and expensive."

Naomi looked over at Jovita. She wasn't in the mood to talk about her mother's date with Steve. "Yeah, he is. To a Japanese restaurant, I think. They're all pretty expensive here in Hong Kong," Naomi replied, grudgingly, then added, "I'll bet he's never had sushi in his life." She smirked. "Mushy peas."

Jovita clapped her hands, "Oh, I can imagine the conversation—she will be telling him all about your life in Japan. He'll be spellbound—impressed—admiring her exotic experiences. Your Mom will say, 'I'll take you there someday—'"

"All right, Jovita, tea's ready. Let's go to the living room."

Jovita jumped off the counter, and her expression became serious. "Naomi, you really need to rethink your whole attitude—"

"There's nothing wrong with my attitude," Naomi cut in coolly. Attitude! Naomi sometimes despised that word. She remembered how her mother lectured about it when they were fighting with each other about being in Japan.

"May I finish?" Jovita countered sternly. Naomi stopped in her tracks. "Naomi, you need to accept the fact that your mom and Steve like each other. And I think they are a nice couple. Everyone does. Steve is good for your mother. He'd be good for you—if you'd give him a chance."

Naomi placed the tray on the table and sat down on the sofa, looking up at her friend. There was nothing but concern and caring in her friend's face. *The last thing I want is to fight with my best friend,* Naomi thought. She sighed. "I know."

Jovita sat down beside Naomi and put a hand on her friend's shoulder. "I know you know."

"Can we just talk about something else, then?" Naomi asked. Jovita nodded. Naomi flicked on the TV, and they sipped their tea, waiting for the pizza to arrive. She thought about how grateful she was for Jovita— and her other special friends like Chen and Grace and the kids at the orphanage—even though they couldn't magically change things to the way she wanted things to be. *Sometimes I think they're all I have,* Naomi thought. The buzzer sounded.

"Pizza!" Jovita cried out and raced to the intercom by the door. Naomi smiled. She knew that she wouldn't be hearing too much talk from Jovita for a while.

⁂   ⁂

"Hi, Naomi. Look! Wai Ming is walking!" Grace said in greeting as Naomi entered the playroom. Naomi smiled down at Grace, who was sitting cross-legged on the floor with two children in her lap. Naomi swooped down on the floor beside Grace and held out her arms. Naomi giggled as three other toddlers headed to Naomi with varying degrees of speed and agility. "They've grown so much in the last month! Amazing!" Naomi heard Grace say.

Naomi nodded in agreement as she cuddled two little girls. Yuk Lin and Sin Ying were both just over a year old and best friends. *They look like two living dolls, just like Mom said,* Naomi decided as she gazed into their round faces, with their deep, velvet brown eyes and rosy apple cheeks. *Two little living Chinese dolls.* Naomi turned to Grace and saw that she, too, was caught up in wonder over the children around her. Naomi glanced furtively at Grace's pregnant stomach. The bump was more pronounced, but still, under the bulk of Grace's winter sweater, it would be hard to say for sure that the girl was pregnant. Grace seemed in especially high spirits today. *I wonder what she'll feel like when she really starts to show,* Naomi thought. *When spring comes, she won't be able to cover things up.* A wave of panic swept over Naomi as she looked at Grace. *What will she do?* Naomi asked herself. When Naomi had told her mother about Grace, Sara had encouraged her daughter to be as supportive as she knew how. But Grace had never been interested in talking about personal things. *Not my business, anyway,* Naomi told herself, and quickly averted her gaze from Grace's stomach.

"Naomi, I want to tell you something," Grace leaned over closer to Naomi as she said this, and Naomi noticed a new excitement in her eyes. "I am thinking of keeping my baby," she whispered. Naomi stared at her in surprise. "I like being with these children. And I've decided I want to keep my own." Grace paused reflectively. "I called my mother and father, and told them I want to see them. I insisted they come here to meet me," Grace went on. "I threatened that I would come over to their house, if they didn't come here." Grace giggled, and Naomi couldn't figure out if they were giggles of joy or nervousness. "I knew they wouldn't want me back in the neighbourhood looking like this!" Grace said with a smile as she patted her stomach. She looked at Naomi with sparkling eyes. "I'm not afraid anymore. I know what I want."

"Grace—that's wonderful," Naomi said a little awkwardly. "Congratulations!" she added in a whisper.

"Thanks," Grace whispered back, and blushed. In her excitement, she reached out and grabbed Naomi's arm.

"I hope everything all works out, then."

"I hope so, too," Grace answered, still in a whisper.

Naomi wanted to be happy for Grace, but something was stopping her from feeling completely assured about Grace and her surprising decision to keep her baby. The way Grace had explained it, things didn't sound too hopeful with her parents.

When Naomi returned to Mother's Love the following week, she went into the playroom as usual looking forward to seeing how Grace was doing. But the girl wasn't there, nor was she there the week after that. When Naomi built up the courage to ask the staff on duty where Grace was, the woman explained that Grace was up in her room, and had been there as well during Naomi's previous visit. Naomi went upstairs and found Grace watching television in the dreary sitting room. The girl looked up with a start when she saw Naomi at the door, then quickly averted her gaze. But Naomi had already noticed Grace's swollen face, and knew that the girl had been crying.

"Do you mind if I come in?" Naomi asked timidly.

Grace pointed to the sofa next to her, then reached for a tissue from the box on the coffee table. Naomi took a seat and looked at Grace, unsure of what to do or say.

"Hi," Grace said, her voice was thick.

"Hi, Grace," Naomi replied. "I've missed you. I only found out today that you were still here. I thought you'd gone, for some reason—"

"Where would I go?" Grace said. She dabbed her eyes with the tissue. "I have no place to go."

"Grace, tell me. What happened? What's wrong?"

Grace looked at the tissue in her hand and began twisting it. "My parents won't let me keep the baby."

"Oh—"

"I'm old enough to keep it," Grace said bitterly. "But they have reminded me that I have no way to take care of the baby. They said they didn't want me to get pregnant, and they don't want me to have the baby—or keep it. They said they will not help me. They will banish me from my family if I try to bring the baby back home."

There was a long pause.

"How could I take care of it myself? I have no where to go with my baby. No money," Grace added in a whisper. She sighed, and looked up at Naomi. "I know adoption is a good thing. But I would like to try to keep—" Grace broke down in sobs and buried her face in her hands.

Naomi moved over and put her arm over Grace's shoulder. "It's a tough decision. I'm so sorry that your parents don't want to help you keep your baby, Grace."

Grace nodded. She looked up and blew her nose. "Oh, Naomi, I want to keep the baby so much! I don't know what to do. It's difficult."

"Yes," Naomi said. "It's not easy—"

"I want to go back to my family," Grace blurted out. Naomi could sense the urgency in the girl's voice. "I miss my little sister especially. I know she misses me."

Naomi listened, surprised at this last revelation. Grace had never spoken about a little sister before. For a fleeting moment, Naomi wondered about this; about what having a little sister must be like. About what the bond must feel like.

"My parents have abandoned me," Grace said. She reached for another tissue. "They won't let me see my sister. They are telling me what to do with my baby. I hate them."

Naomi gently squeezed Grace's shoulder. Again, Naomi found herself comparing the girl's situation to her own. *I can kind of relate to that— abandonment,* Naomi let herself think, *with Mom deciding to spend her time with Steve instead of me.* But as soon as she allowed herself to think it, Naomi dropped the thought, feeling ashamed. *There's no comparison between what is happening between Grace and her parents and what's going on between me and Mom.*

Grace blew her nose again and straightened up in the chair. "So, I am thinking about giving up my baby for adoption, like a lot of pregnant girls do. Edith has talked to me about it. She says I am going to give my baby a wonderful life, with people who want to have my baby so much— I have no idea how much, she says. I know that's a good thing." Grace reached for another tissue and wiped her eyes. "It might be a local Chinese couple, or it could be someone from far away; Australia, America, Canada—who knows?"

"Wherever your baby goes, it will be loved, that's for sure," Naomi said, trying to console her friend.

"I know," Grace replied. Naomi thought the girl was going to regain her composure with this hopeful thought, but then Grace's face crumpled again and she sobbed, "But why can't I be the one—" At that, Grace rose from the sofa and walked blindly into the corridor and towards her room. Naomi rose up and followed her, but Grace shook her off. "No, Naomi. I'll be okay. I just need a little more time to get over this. I'll try to be back downstairs next week. See you." Grace entered her room and closed the door.

Naomi stood silently in the hall for several moments before deciding to visit the children as planned. But she didn't stay long. She was feeling miserable about Grace, and about so many other things, too. She knew she wasn't being very good company that day. As she walked home, her mind was swimming: *Mom and Steve—Jovita and everyone else pressuring me to like him, including Baba and Gigi, Grace and her baby and her family—*Naomi began. *All these amazing little kids, so desperate for my affection, because there's no one else in their lives to give it to them.* Naomi thought about Chen. *Even Chen has some kind of bad secret in his past, I know he does. I can tell. It's too sad for him to even talk about, it seems.*

Naomi stomped her feet there on the sidewalk, trying to banish the demons. *Try to think of something fun,* she told herself. After a few moments, she answered herself; "I know—Macau!" *Mom and I are going to Macau for Easter. Another new place. Just me and Mom on another little adventure.* Naomi forced herself to think of the things she had read about in the Macau guidebook she had received on her birthday: *Hac Sa Beach, egg tarts, African chicken—*

And then, from somewhere deep inside her heart, she heard a whisper: *You can run, but you cannot hide.*

Macau is comprised of a six-square-mile area on the mainland of China and the adjacent islands of Taipa and Coloane. Formerly a colony of Portugal, Macau became a Special Administrative Region of the People's Republic of China on December 20, 1999. Macau is a unique mix of East and West; Baroque churches and Chinese temples, Portuguese restaurants and traditional Chinese medicine dispensaries. In Macau, Easter is as celebrated as the Chinese Lunar New Year.

—Macau Tourist Authority

Sara looked up from her newspaper and stared out the window of the hovercraft. "So quick. Only an hour. I can't believe it's taken us more than seven months to finally make a visit to Macau."

"Jovita says it's like a piece of Portugal in China, with street signs and statues of Portuguese explorers. And she says Macanese food tastes great!" Naomi stated enthusiastically.

"Oh, I know," Sara replied. "Macanese cuisine is a blend of Chinese, Portuguese and African cooking. Portugal had colonies all over the world."

They filed through the immigration and customs areas and caught a taxi to their hotel, a converted Portuguese fortress, over 400 years old, called The Poussada.

"This place is gorgeous!" exclaimed Sara as they climbed the hotel's stairway, which had been built into the wall of the fortress. On each side of the stairs, running down its length, was a rivulet of water. The effect of this water feature, with its stony, damp smell and burbling sound, was instantly relaxing.

Naomi and Sara were shown to their room, which had elegant four-poster beds and multicoloured tile floors. Naomi dropped her bag on one of the beds and headed for the balcony which was shaded by a large tree. She looked out over the swimming pool and the wide expanse of water farther along, coloured brown by the silt in the Pearl River delta. On the other side, at the water's edge, were a few large buildings with a row of green hills beyond. It was a peaceful contrast to the view from her bedroom window in Happy Valley. Naomi stood silently, taking in the unfamiliar scene. She watched a ferry boat ply the river, crowded with tourists from mainland China. Naomi knew China was not far away. She looked at the buildings on the other side of the river. "I wonder if that's China over there."

Sara stepped onto the balcony. "I think you're right, Naomi. Taipa and Coloane aren't in that direction, so that must be the mainland. Let's say we have some lunch and then head out to the border with China. I hear it's supposed to be an interesting place."

They went to the patio restaurant and sat down at a table under an enormous old tree. The waiter handed out large menus and they settled down to choose from the tantalizing selection of Portuguese, Macanese, and Chinese dishes. As Naomi decided on the grilled sardines and a salad, she closed the cover of the menu and began reading about the history of the hotel. The fortress had been built centuries ago, when a Catholic Missionary named Saint Francis Xavier was living in Macau. Naomi's eyebrows shot up in surprise and she continued to read. She wondered if it was the same person after whom the university in Nova Scotia was named.

"Mom! It says here that a piece of Saint Frances Xavier's arm bone is in Macau!

"Seriously?"

Naomi pointed to the menu. "That's what it says. It's in a little church on Coloane Island." She looked up at her mother. "Mom—we have to go there."

"It seems hard to believe. But sure—we'll go check it out," replied Sara.

After lunch, Naomi and her mother took a taxi to the border with China. As Naomi stepped out of the taxi, she looked up at a large gated structure, lined with the blue and white tiles that were so distinctly Portuguese. On either side of the gated area was a concertina-wire fence; at Naomi's left, people were walking into Macau, and on the right, the movement of people was in the opposite direction.

Naomi walked into an area the jutted out beyond the gates and over to the fence, watching people file out of Macau loaded down with boxes and bundles of all kinds. She looked at her mother and mischievously stuck her fingers through the wire fence. "I'm in China, now, without a visa!"

Sara laughed and took a picture of Naomi at the fence. They bought drinks and sat on a bench to watch some artists do a brisk business selling paintings on the sidewalk in front of the gates.

"Things seem to move slower here in Macau, compared to Hong Kong," said Sara.

"I was thinking the same thing."

Sara looked at Naomi. "Yeah. In Hong Kong I sometimes feel that we just don't get time to really *see* things. Everyone is so busy with their own lives. It can be a real treadmill." She grinned. "Now, here in Macau, we can do neat things like go searching for buried—or ought-to-be-buried—treasure. Like a piece of a saint's arm bone! Won't that be fun." Sara reached over and ruffled her daughter's hair affectionately. "Shall we head over to Coloane now and see what we can find?"

Sara flagged down another taxi which took them over a long bridge to the island of Taipa and across a causeway to Coloane. The island of Coloane was, unlike Taipa and peninsular Macau, very green and quite undeveloped. After 10 minutes, the taxi dropped them off in a small village square. Naomi and Sara followed their noses down a back alley and soon found themselves looking up at a quaint European-looking church, painted yellow with blue and white trim. It was at the top of a cobble-stone square which had a fountain at the opposite end. On either side were two busy open air cafes serving lunches and a delicious assortment of Chinese and Portuguese pastries.

"I think this must be the place. I'm going in," Naomi said excitedly, and stepped through the doors of the pristine little church. It looked even smaller from the inside; there were only two columns of seven pews, and the altar was so small that it seemed miniature. Naomi noticed an elderly man dressed in a white robe sitting alone in the first pew. He had a long flowing white beard and glasses with thick black frames. He turned and smiled at Naomi.

Naomi took a step forward. "Hello, I'm sorry to trouble you. I'm looking for—my guide book says that there is a—an arm bone—in this church—" Naomi said, suddenly feeling more than a little foolish.

The man stood up slowly and nodded. "You are looking for the arm bone of Saint Francis Xavier. It was kept right here for many years," he said, pointing towards the small altar. "But I'm afraid that it is no longer available for public viewing."

"Oh," Naomi replied, disappointed. She stood facing the old man for a few seconds, hoping that he might change his mind. "Well, thank you very much. Sorry for troubling you." Naomi bowed and headed back out of the church to find her mother. She gazed across the bright sunlit square and spotted Sara standing at the opposite end, looking at some more of the paintings that Naomi now realized were commonly sold by visiting artists from the mainland. Naomi trotted up to her mother, interested to see what had caught her mother's attention.

"Mom—" Naomi began, then stopped. Her mother was staring intently at a painting of a young Chinese girl, wearing an orange scarf on her head, tied in a neat bow under her chin, and wearing a red quilted winter coat.

"She's lovely, isn't she," said Sara. "I think she comes from northern China."

Naomi looked for a long time at the girl's face, trying to think what was in her mother's mind. The girl in the picture was looking out at the viewer with an enigmatic expression, showing neither delight nor sorrow. Naomi's thoughts turned to the children at Mother's Love, and all their flushed, excited faces. *They are always so cheerful whenever I'm with them,* she thought, then looked again at the girl in the painting. "I think the girl is lonely," she commented. Sara nodded in agreement. Naomi scanned the other paintings, all different styles; from oil paintings of contemporary life to the traditional scroll-paintings of Chinese mountain scenes and running horses. But Naomi was repeatedly drawn back to the picture of the little girl.

Sara turned to Naomi. "So, what did you find out about the arm bone? Is it there?"

"No. The priest in there told me it's not available for viewing," Naomi replied.

"Oh, that's too bad, Naomi. I hope you're not too disappointed."

Naomi shook her head. "No—not really. It was a bit of a wild goose chase, but if we hadn't come here, we wouldn't have seen this amazing bit of Portugal right here in Macau."

Sara looked at her watch. "Well there's plenty more to see, after breaktime."

After some tea and coffee and Portuguese egg tarts at the cafe in the square, Naomi and her mother caught a bus back to central Macau. They spent several hours wandering the cobbled pedestrian area from Leal Senado Square, where the former colonial parliament building was located, along streets lined with shops, to the famous facade of St. Paul's Cathedral. Known as the landmark of Macau, the front wall of the Cathedral was the only thing standing after the 400-year-old church had been burned to the ground years ago.

Naomi and her mother climbed up the steps to the church facade and then over to another fortress on a nearby hill. They looked over the ramparts, and saw the crowded streets of Macau beneath them, packed tightly into the space confined by water on three sides. "What an amazing place! There's so much life down there—in such a small space. I admit I had no idea what to expect, but Macau is unique. Steve was right," Sara said, and she looked over at Naomi. "Steve had asked if he could meet us here today," she added absently.

"Is he coming?" Naomi asked.

Sara smiled and shook her head. "No, he's not. I thought you might feel a little—uncomfortable—the three of us walking around Macau together," she said. "Although you needn't be. Maybe we can do something, just the three of us—go for hike, or something—someday?"

Naomi grimaced.

Sara looked hard at her daughter. "Don't you think it's fun to have someone else around? You have your girlfriends—"

Naomi glared at her mother, suddenly very angry and defensive. "Oh, so you have a boyfriend now, and my company is no longer required—"

Sara glanced up in alarm, and grabbed Naomi's arm. "Naomi, I didn't mean that. As you well know!"

"Sounds like you did to me!" Naomi shot back.

"Naomi. Look. I'm glad you don't mind Steve and I going out from time to time," Sara began earnestly. "Or, at least, I think you don't. But— I thought—it would be nice to do things together. The three of us."

"Don't I have a say in this?" asked Naomi sarcastically.

Sara sighed. "Okay, Naomi. I appreciate that you realize your mom wants to have friends—just as you do. But I guess I can't force you to be Steve's friend." There was a hint of bitterness in her voice when she added, "But maybe it wouldn't hurt you to be nice to him, and you would see he really is someone worth knowing."

Naomi turned on her heel and walked down the hill towards the hotel, no longer interested in sightseeing or eating. "I'm going back to the hotel," she called out over her shoulder without breaking stride. Sara started to follow her, then stopped. She watched her daughter's figure stomp down the hill and disappear around a corner.

It was two hours later when Sara returned to the hotel, expecting to find Naomi. But Naomi wasn't in the room, the patio cafe, or the swimming pool. Sara nervously paced the hotel room, wondering what her sometimes impulsive and stubborn daughter was doing. Her heart leapt with relief when she heard the key turn in the lock and watched her daughter enter, carrying a large, flat object.

Naomi came into the room and looked at her mother with a guilty expression. She put the package on the bed. A tear rolled down her cheek. Sara went to Naomi and put an arm over her shoulder. "What is it, honey?"

Naomi put her head on her mother's shoulder and soon her shoulders were shaking with silent sobs. "I'm sorry, Mom. I know you have a life. I know Steve is a great guy. I know that I'm not being very friendly. But— it's—hard."

Sara turned Naomi toward her and looked at her in the eyes. "Why? What's wrong, Naomi? Tell me. What's wrong?"

Naomi shook her head and hugged her mother. "I'm just sorry. I'm sorry that I walked away from you today. That was stupid. I'm not being very grown up—"

Sara smiled and gave Naomi a hug. "But you will always be my baby."

Naomi giggled through her tears, and then reached for a tissue from the dressing table and blew her nose. She pointed to the package she had placed on the bed. "I bought this for you, Mom."

"Oh, Naomi," Sara said, her eyes wide with surprise. "You didn't need to do that. I didn't get you anything—yet." Sara sat down on the bed and began unwrapping the package. She put her hand to her mouth as the surprise was revealed. It was the painting of the little Chinese girl.

"Naomi, it's lovely. I really do love it. And I would never have bought it for myself." She gave Naomi a hug and a kiss. "What a lovely, thoughtful present."

Naomi looked at her mother and smiled. "I like the picture, too. I just thought this little girl needed a home," Naomi replied, then grinned. "I think, maybe, I bought it for both of us. You can call it an Easter present. Or you can call it a Mother's Day present—in advance."

十六

Buddha's birthday has great importance for Hong Kong's Buddhist community. Many worshippers visit the Po Lin Monastery on Lantau Island, home to the world's largest, seated, outdoor bronze Buddha. The Buddha Statue weighs over 202 tons and rises 26 metres above its platform on the Ngong Ping Plateau.

— Hong Kong Tourist Authority

"Honey, would you like to go for a hike tomorrow?" Sara asked Naomi as they sat over bowls of noodles after a visit to Mother's Love.

"That would be nice," Naomi replied. "I have an idea. We could go to see the giant Buddha and Po Lin Monastery over on Lantau Island. Then we could go hike up Lantau Peak. It's the second highest mountain in Hong Kong, and right next to the Buddha statue. Chen told me it's Buddha's birthday—"

"Yes, it is," Sara said, a little awkwardly. "Actually, that's exactly what I had in mind. Or, what Steve had in mind—"

Back to Steve again!

"Steve and his friends have organized a hike to Lantau Peak and then a junk trip around Lantau Island afterwards. There will be a lot of the other kids your age—"

"Can I bring Jovita?" she asked.

"If you like," Sara replied. She took Naomi's hand in hers, "But I thought we could just try something—just you and me and Steve—"

"But you said there will be all of his friends there."

Sara nodded and smiled. Naomi could see a hint of nervousness in her mother's manner. "I know. But, I mean, the three of us, try to do something together. I think, with Jovita along, you won't pay much attention to us—" Sara chuckled nervously.

Naomi looked at her mother in surprise. "You mean, *you* won't pay much attention to *me*, with Steve around."

Sara shook her head. "Naomi, Steve wants to get to know you better. We've talked about this before. I thought you were going to give him a chance—"

"Okay. I'll go," Naomi said, and saw her mother's face brighten instantly. "If it'll make *you* happy."

"Well, wait a minute, Naomi," Sara replied. "I want you to want to do this. Of course it would make me happy if all three of us could get along, but I care about you, Naomi. What will make you happy?"

Naomi looked at her mother's face, so full of concern. Naomi had no idea how to respond to that simple question. She didn't even want to think about it. Naomi knew by now that, as soon as she started thinking about the idea of a romantic interest in her mother's life, her stomach tightened and her arms felt heavy. Over the last few weeks, she had been trying to be more accepting of Steve, but real life was proving to be a little more difficult. And in all this time, Naomi had chosen to skirt the issue and focus instead on other things, like Grace and the children at the orphanage, or Chen's *tai chi* lessons, or school. Naomi's thoughts were diverted to Grace and the terrible setback she was forced to face when her parents told her she could not keep her baby. Grace's sorrowful, lonely face entered her mind. Naomi sighed, *Why does life have to get so complicated?* she asked herself. *Why is there so much loneliness?*

"Naomi, please tell me. What would make you happy?" Sara's voice interrupted Naomi's thoughts.

Naomi shrugged her shoulders. "I don't know."

Early the next day, Naomi was staring up at an enormous golden Buddha. Behind it stood the outline of Lantau Peak, shrouded in a morning mist.

"It's a good day for a climb—a little overcast," Steve said eagerly. He turned to Naomi. "Did you know that you are looking at the world's largest outdoor seated bronze Buddha?" He laughed and looked over at Sara, "I suppose, if you add enough adjectives, every city can claim fame with the world's biggest, best, something-or-other."

Sara laughed along with him. "Yeah, I see what you mean. It *is* impressive, though.

After a group photo at the Buddha, the group set off on the two-hour trek to the top of Lantau Peak. The morning mist had worn off before they had reached the top, but the scattered clouds prevented the weather from getting dangerously hot. After a break at the peak, it was a short climb down to the road, where a chartered bus was waiting to take the group to the town of Mui Wo, where they waited, chatting and laughing, for the ferry that would take them back to Hong Kong Island.

"I'm famished," Naomi heard someone say.

Soon, a large junk appeared from around the corner and made it's way towards the pier. Naomi, her mother, and Steve took a place in line to board the junk. Naomi felt a little nervous again because, once on board the junk, Naomi knew she would have to try her best to mingle with Steve and his British friends. Naomi found herself at the bow of the boat with her mother and a few others, while Steve went to get some drinks.

"Well, did you enjoy your exercise today?" someone asked.

Naomi turned to see a tall, distinguished-looking older man sitting on the bench, in immaculate white pants and a navy blazer. Naomi was sure she hadn't seen him on the hiking trail—she would have certainly noticed.

"We sure did," Sara declared and laughed. "But you don't look like you came dressed for a hike up Lantau Peak."

The man looked at Sara and Naomi, and then turned his gaze to the island they were now steering away from. He nodded. "Quite right. I'm not of that ilk. I prefer to stay down in the tea rooms and in and around the monastery. I'll leave the heavy work to you younger lot."

Sara asked, "Are any of your kids here?"

The man shook his head slowly and forced a chuckle. "Goodness, no. They moved back to England a long time ago, with my ex-wife. I enjoy coming along on these excursions that some of the British expat families plan from time to time." The man smiled a crooked smile. "It gets me out—even if I don't get up those hills."

"How long have you lived in Hong Kong?" Sara asked.

"Over 20 years," the man replied. "I came out from London, when this place was a fine British colony. Although certainly not 'The Jewel in the Crown'."

Naomi wondered what he meant, but felt too intimidated to ask.

"That's a long time. You must enjoy it here then," Sara commented.

"Oh, Hong Kong. Money, passports, ancestor worship. That's all there is to it, really." The man sighed with, what seemed to Naomi, an air of boredom. "But it'll do."

Naomi decided she didn't like this man.

"Tell us what the Handover was like. That must have been very interesting," Sara said.

The man laughed, "Oh, it was. I watched from the bar at the Metropole Hotel in Hanoi, Vietnam. Lovely, it was. A very faux-British affair," he added, waving his hand in the air and exaggerating his British accent.

"The Handover—faux-British?" Sara asked, puzzled.

"No—the bar in Hanoi," the man answered with a sigh. He rolled his eyes, then continued, "Well, when I returned to Hong Kong after my sojourn I was told that it rained a lot. But things haven't really changed all that much—for us expats, in any event." The man suddenly stood up. "Nice meeting you lot—"

"Sara—and my daughter, Naomi," Sara replied hastily.

"Charmed. Enjoy your time in Hong Kong. I just noticed a colleague over there with whom I must speak. If you'll excuse me." The man walked back to the bar, helped himself to a drink and then walked up to a group of people who were standing in a tight circle at the opposite end of the junk. Sara and Naomi waited in silence for Steve to return.

It was early evening before Naomi, Sara and Steve returned to Happy Valley.

"Thanks so much for organizing the day," Sara said, as they rode the elevator up to their floor. "Would you like to come in for a cup of tea, or something?"

Steve smiled and shook his head. "I'd love to, but that hike has done me in. I'm getting old," he said with a grimace. He turned to Naomi and asked, "Did you enjoy yourself, Naomi? I noticed you talking with old Rupert." Steve glanced at Sara. "Whatever he said, you must take it with a grain of salt. He's been here forever. Too long, maybe." Naomi noticed Steve's smile was fading. "He's okay, if you understand where he's coming from. He's an old colonial type, in the mold of Somerset Maugham. A real piece of work, he is. He was different, though, once—before he got divorced and his wife and kids moved back to the UK and left him here all alone."

As Naomi and her mother unpacked from the day's excursion, Naomi thought of 'Old Rupert', as Steve called him. *I don't know him, but I don't like him,* Naomi thought. Naomi recounted the conversation they'd had on the junk. *He's lonely,* Naomi realized, *and that has made him bitter. That's what happens when you take chances. Steve will be like that someday. And I don't want Mom to end up like that, too.* Suddenly, Naomi decided she needed to say something to her mother. She walked into Sara's room, and saw her mother throwing some laundry on her bed. "I'm tired of Steve and his snooty British friends," Naomi stated defiantly from the doorway. She glared at her mother and said "And I HATE mushy peas!"

Sara looked up from the pile of hiking gear and towels on her bed, eyes wide. She was surprised and mystified by her daughter's sudden angry outburst. She turned to her daughter and put her hands on her hips. "You're *tired* of Steve? Well, that's very *snooty* of you, don't you think?" she replied and then added. "I know who you're talking about, Naomi. You might consider that a part of what that man says has to do with the fact that he seems—to me, anyway—to not have a lot going for him." Sara and Naomi stared each other down. "And anyway, Steve's not like that man. Steve's from Yorkshire."

"So? What's that supposed to mean," Naomi shot back.

"Yorkshire is like Manitoba. Except it's in England. People there are very down-to-earth," Sara answered. "If you cared to know Steve better, you would see what a wonderful man he is." She raised her arms as she cried out, "Is it because I love him that you have decided to hate him?"

Sara and Naomi both froze, staring at each other. Naomi stood stiffly as she watched her mother put her hand to her mouth and slowly move across the room towards her. Sara put her hands on Naomi's shoulders, but stared down at the floor for several moments before finally looking up into Naomi's eyes. Naomi could feel her throat becoming dry.

As Sara looked at Naomi, her eyes filled with tears. Slowly, the slightest smile began to form on her lips, and she began to speak. "Naomi. I think I do. I think I do love Steve." It was almost a whisper.

Naomi began to shake. Her eyes stung with tears and her lips trembled. "Please, Mom. Don't—"

Sara's eyes widened in fear. She had never seen her daughter so afraid. She clutched her daughter's shoulders. "Naomi, what is it? What's wrong? What are you afraid of? What's wrong Naomi. This time please tell me. You must talk to me!"

"I—I just don't know what will happen if you—"

"If I what?"

"If you keep dating him, or something. Maybe he'll leave you."

Sara nodded dismissively. "I can handle that. As you will too, someday. It's all a part of growing up. It's a part of—life, Naomi."

"I already know about it. Dad already left me," Naomi's legs buckled and she began to cry. "Maybe you—"

Sara wrapped her arms around Naomi, rocking her for several moments. Then Sara began to speak, slowly, as the realization of her daughter's fear took hold. "Is this what you are thinking? That I will leave you? No, Naomi, I never will. I will always be with you."

Naomi wiped away tears from her eyes. "Please. Don't. I'll take care of you. You won't ever be alone, if you—just—stay with me—"

Sara looked into Naomi's eyes and stroked her hair gently. "Naomi. I'm never going to leave you—like you think your dad did. Got married and started another family for himself. You didn't think that, did you? You didn't think I was going to leave you if—" Sara shook her head. "Look. I don't know what the future has in store for any of us. But I do know this: You and I will always be together. You and I will be together until *you* decide to leave *me*. We're a team, remember?" Sara gave her daughter another tight squeeze. As they embraced, Naomi couldn't see the grief etched in her mother's face.

Tuen Ng (the Dragon Boat Festival) memorializes the life of the poet Chu Yuan, who drowned the 5th day of the 5th lunar month in the year 277 B.C. It is thought that the vilagers, who were unable to save him, threw bamboo leaves stuffed with rice into the water in order to prevent the hungry fish from eating their beloved poet. The boat races on this day attract large crowds. Sixteen rowers paddle the long and slender canoes, which are decorated with a dragon's head at the front.

—Hong Kong Tourist Authority

Naomi didn't see Steve very often after that day on the junk. It had taken Naomi a little time before she realized that he and her mother were not dating anymore, and that he was no longer finding excuses to drop by their apartment. Only once did Naomi run into him, in the elevator on the way home from Jovita's place one evening. In a pleasant way, he had asked Naomi how school was going, but it had felt awkward. However, Naomi refused to give the new situation much thought; the school year was winding down, and both she and her mother were busy preparing for final exams. *I'm too busy to wonder what the story is with Steve,* Naomi would sometimes tell herself. *And so is Mom.*

With only weeks to spare, Sara had decided to try out for the school's staff Dragon Boat team. Each year, teachers from across Hong Kong participated in the Dragon Boat races held at Sai Kung, which was one of the most prestigious and competitive events of the school year. Naomi noticed with a sense of awe and bewilderment how her mother threw herself into training for the races. Each morning, Naomi would hear her mother slip out the door for a jog at 5:30. Some evenings, she swam laps and did weight-training exercises at the community centre. During these evenings Naomi was alone at home, and she would try to concentrate on her upcoming exams. But there was no mistaking the transformation; the apartment had become a quiet and lonely place. Several times over the last few weeks, Naomi had found herself sitting on the sofa among stacks of books, staring out the window—as she often did—and that's when the realization would start to creep in. Although nothing had ever been spoken between Naomi and her mother about it, Naomi was beginning to understand the truth; that her mother had ended her relationship with Steve—and it was because of her.

Now, as Naomi stepped out onto the street on the morning of the Dragon Boat races, the air seemed to have a certain stillness. It seemed to hover about her body, and the whole city. Sara was already making her way to Sai Kung for a final practise before the race. School had ended last week; exams were complete and Naomi knew she had done well. Jovita had left the night before to spend a few weeks with her relatives in Vancouver. Naomi headed to the neighbourhood coffee shop, ordered an iced cocoa, and looked around at the customers, who were sitting mostly in pairs and chatting animatedly. Feeling listless and lonely, Naomi headed out the door, stopping in front of the small park to watch Chen practise *tai chi*. She waved, and stood watching him for a long time. She breathed deeply as Chen had taught her, hoping to find, as Chen would say, her 'balance', or inner calm.

Back at home, Naomi went to her bedroom and lay down. She stared at the ceiling, listening to the silence in the apartment, and the faint sound of traffic from the street below. Naomi turned to the stack of books on her bedside table and reached for the book that Chen had given her. Naomi read a few lines on one page, then flipped to another. With a sigh and a grimace, Naomi returned the book to the pile. "I don't understand," she said. She got up and headed into the living room, turned on the air-conditioner, then grabbed the TV remote control on her way to the sofa. She turned on the English-language morning news broadcast, which was in the middle of a segment on the Dragon Boat festivities taking place all over Hong Kong. Naomi looked at her watch, knowing that she would soon have to leave in order to get to Sai Kung in time to see her mother race.

"The weather promises to co-operate for the Dragon Boat Festival. It will be a great day for the Dragon Boat races; sunny and hot, with occasional scattered clouds. It should be noted, however, that Typhoon Signal One was hoisted this morning at 5:30. Here's more from the Hong Kong Weather Observatory—"

Naomi's eyebrows shot up in surprise. She had heard a lot about the famous typhoons of South China. Although the typhoon season can start as early as April, it had been a good year so far, and no typhoons had come near Hong Kong. The news broadcast switched over to a man standing in front of weather map of the South China Sea, which was marked with barometric pressure lines. He was pointing to a series of circles concentrated over the sea near the coast of China.

"Tropical depression Milton is now centred west of the Philippines," the official from the Hong Kong Weather Observatory explained. "It is moving slowly towards the South China Coast, in the direction of Hainan Island. If Milton continues along this trajectory, Hong Kong can expect to experience showers and wind gusts from early tomorrow morning. At this time we don't expect that it will be necessary to hoist the Typhoon Signal Three."

Naomi nodded thoughtfully and shut off the television. *So this is the calm before the storm. I wouldn't mind being caught in a real South China Sea typhoon. Maybe Milton will bring some action,* Naomi mused as she headed out the door.

At Sai Kung, Naomi following the throng of happy families to the beach, which was already swarming with people. Along the shore, Naomi saw eight boats in the water and rows of marker buoys in columns heading out into the water away from the beach. Naomi walked along, looking for the familiar orange and blue T-shirts of the Dragon Boat team from her school.

"Naomi! Naomi!"

Naomi saw her mother waving, and jogged over to gave her mother a big hug. "Hi, Mom. Here's an energy hug from me."

Sara was breathing hard and her eyes were wide with excitement. "We've had two practise runs an hour ago. I think it's tired me out!"

"When's your first race?"

"Ten o'clock. We're in the second heat," replied Sara. She draped her arm over her daughter's shoulders. "I do need some energy." Someone began to talk over the loudspeaker, and people began to walk towards the shore again. "The first race is about to start," Sara said with excitement.

Naomi could see eight boats manoeuvring out at the starting line. As the last of the Dragon Boats got into position, the starter's pistol went off, immediately followed by the rhythmic beats from the drums. At the front of each Dragon Boat, the coxswain sat beating a drum, exhorting the crew to row faster and harder. Soon, some of the boats began to pull ahead, and the race was narrowed down to three. A horn blasted as two boats cleared the finish line and some groups of people began to cheer.

May yelled over the din. "Come on Sara, we're next."

Sara turned to her daughter. Naomi could feel her mother's arms shaking as she hugged her. "You can do it, Mom!" Naomi said.

Sara and the other racers stepped into their boat and Naomi helped push it back into the water. With a final wave to her mother, Naomi watched as the boat moved smoothly towards the starting line. *You look good,* Naomi thought, but surveyed the competition and had to admit that her mother's team would have to give it all they had if they were going to win. Naomi watched with growing nervousness as the boats began to manoeuvre into starting position. As the final boat managed to pull itself up to the line, the pistol went off and immediately the cheering and drumbeats began in earnest once again.

"Go! Go!" Naomi cried out. The line of boats began to pull apart, her mom's boat among the leaders. Naomi watched with increasing hope as the boat pulled farther ahead. Within seconds, two other Dragon Boats surged forward, passing the one she was cheering for. "GO! GO! GO!" Naomi screamed, jumping up and down with the other supporters.

Naomi turned and glanced down the beach at the crowd. Her face froze. Steve was standing only a few metres away from her. He was looking at her with a big grin on his face, and gave her the thumbs up sign. Naomi's face burned with embarrassment. She smiled lamely, then stepped forward into the water, trying to focus on the race. But she couldn't. There was something she needed to know. Slowly, Naomi turned her head to see if she could spot Steve through the crowd once again. When she saw him, she knew she had not been mistaken; there was a woman standing next to Steve and it was clear they were together. The woman had her hand on Steve's arm. Naomi turned her face back towards the sea, and to the boat race. But she couldn't see anything. Her eyes blurred and her ears seemed to be ringing.

"COME ON!" someone behind Naomi shouted. With a start, she saw that the leading boats were reaching the finish line, and Naomi could clearly make out her mother's face, taut with exertion. The drum beats were quickening and the rowers were increasing their speed, giving every last ounce of effort they had. Sara's boat began to pull ahead again, with only twenty metres to the finish line. "YES!" Naomi yelled out, thrusting her arms in the air. At that moment, the boat from the far right came even with Sara's boat as they crossed the finish line. Cheers went up at both ends of the beach. Naomi's jaw dropped, and she looked towards the marquis, to see what the announcement would be.

"The winner is—Kowloon Junior School!"

Cheers and applause erupted at the opposite end of the beach and Naomi could see the winning rowers hugging each other as their boat glided towards the sand. Naomi waded out into the water to help bring in her team's boat. Amid cheers and clapping, Naomi helped her mother out of the boat.

"Second place, Mom. Not bad," Naomi said.

"You bet that's not bad. We get to advance to the next stage," replied Sara, breathless. Naomi could see how thrilled her mother was, even in defeat.

"Steve's here," Naomi blurted out.

"He is!" Sara cried out with a surprised smile. Her eyes widened and she grabbed Naomi's shoulders for support as she continued to breath hard. "Where is he?"

"He's with someone." Naomi was looking at the sand. She didn't want to see the look in her mother's eyes.

"He is?" Naomi heard her mother say again, this time in a small voice. There was a silence between them as the rest of the crowd continued to laugh and cheer. Then Sara shrugged. "Well, anyway, let's get me a drink. Your mother needs fluids. Our next race is coming up soon."

It wasn't long before Naomi was once again giving her mother a last-minute good luck hug. To Naomi's delight and relief, Sara and her team won the race and advanced to another round. But their luck ended there; they finished in sixth place and Naomi and her mother watched the final race together with the rest of the school's supporters. The trophy was awarded to Kowloon Junior School for a second consecutive year.

"Well, they deserve it. They are unbeatable," Sara said matter-of-factly, as the winning team walked onto the podium. The crowd roared and clapped their admiration. Naomi looked up at the sky and noticed it had become dark with heavy storm clouds. The wind had begun to pick up, too, flapping the walls of the marquis and adding to the din.

"Sara, are you coming out with us tonight?" shouted one of her team-mates. Sara turned to look at Naomi.

"You go ahead, Mom."

"But what'll you do tonight?"

"Mom. Don't worry about me," Naomi said, then added. "You go. Have a good time."

Sara smiled. "All right, then. I will."

Naomi waved goodbye to the excited and exhausted group of revellers and headed back to the bus terminus. It was time for dinner, and Naomi thought about what was in the fridge, but then the image of Steve and his lady friend entered her mind again, followed by the disappointment in her mother's voice when she had said that Steve was not alone. Naomi sighed. She approached the line of buses that would soon be taking people back to all parts of Hong Kong, and headed for the one to Happy Valley. But, as Naomi neared the bus door, she decided to keep walking, and instead got on the bus to Hollywood Road.

eighteen

Yield to overcome; bend to be straight.

—Chinese Proverb

F at raindrops had begun to fall by the time Naomi stepped off the bus in Mid-levels, and she jogged the block from the bus stop to Chen's antique store, trying to avoid getting soaked. She smiled, remembering something her grandfather always liked to say to her when it was rainy: Walk between the raindrops. As Naomi passed an elegant apartment block with floor-to-ceiling windows, she noticed a sign posted in the lobby: Typhoon Signal Three is Hoisted. She ran to Chen's shop, and pushed the door open brusquely. The bell by the door clanged and Naomi could see Chen look up from his place behind the counter.

"Naomi!" Chen said, smiling warmly. "Welcome in from the rain. What brings you here on Tuen Ng Festival?"

Naomi stood by the door and shook off her rucksack before stepping into the shop. "I was in Sai Kung today, watching the schoolteachers' Dragon Boat races," Naomi replied. "Mom was in it. Our school did pretty good. We made it through a few heats. But Kowloon Junior School won the final race. Mom's out celebrating now with her team."

Chen nodded, impressed. "That's very good. And what a wonderful memory of your mother's stay in Hong Kong—to be in a Dragon Boat race. It's a lot of effort. People practise for months for the Dragon Boat races," Chen said. "Good for her."

Naomi nodded, once again reminded of her mother's disciplined training for the races after Steve had stopped coming around—and of the lonely evenings in the apartment cramming for her own exams. Pangs of guilt and loneliness began to resurface.

Chen motioned Naomi over to the back room. "Come have some hot tea."

"That would be great, Chen," Naomi replied, and followed him into the small back room, taking a seat at the table.

"What are your plans for the summer holidays, Naomi?" Chen asked as he opened a tin of tea grounds and spooned them into a small teapot.

"We'll go home for the summer. But we'll be back in late August. Mom has a two-year contract with the school," Naomi replied.

"You must be looking forward to that; going home to see your grandparents—your Baba and Gigi," Chen said with a smile.

Naomi nodded. "I am, but, for a while, Mom and I talked about travelling somewhere in China. Or maybe somewhere else in Asia for a bit—like Nepal or Vietnam. Everyone says how lovely they are. My friend Jovita went hiking in Nepal last summer."

"Where's Jovita today?" Chen asked.

Naomi sighed. "She's gone to Canada to spend the summer with relatives. She left yesterday. I'm kind of here all by myself."

Chen looked over at Naomi, then turned back to the teapot. He poured some boiling water into the pot and placed the lid on top. He then put two tiny handleless teacups next to the pot and brought the tray over to the table. "Well, perhaps it's just as well that you are going back to Canada, then. You must miss your family." Chen took a seat on the stool next to Naomi. "As for exploring the wonders of Asia—there's always next summer. After all, China is a part of your life now."

"You're right. There's always next summer." Naomi smiled and bowed slightly as Chen poured a cup of tea and placed it in front of her. "But we do miss Canada." Naomi stared into her teacup. "I think, actually, that Mom misses Canada more than me. Sometimes."

Chen nodded, looking intently at the girl sitting next to him. "I can imagine. Even though I know you have made many good friends here, it is important to stay as close as possible with family. Family is important. It is said that family is especially important in the Chinese culture, but I think it must be the same in all cultures—all over the world."

Naomi watched Chen take a sip from his small teacup, and he continued, "Traditionally, in Chinese culture, one of the most important responsibilities is for a child to obey and respect their parents' wishes. No matter what."

"Filial piety," Naomi said quietly, nodding. She'd learned that term while reading her book about Chinese horoscopes.

"Yes. In English you call it 'filial piety'," Chen said. "You observed this yourself, Naomi, when you went to Japan to live your mother, and then when you returned to Canada a year later. In both cases, you didn't really want to go, you told me—"

"Yes, it's true," Naomi chuckled, "But I didn't really have any choice. I was only 12 years old. Besides, looking back, I'm glad I went—"

"Perhaps, you can consider that it was your destiny to go to Japan—and then later, to come to Hong Kong," Chen said, "Imagine what obstacle you would have put in the path of your own destiny, if you had chosen not to respect your mother's wishes."

"Well, I wouldn't be sitting here talking to you, Chen. That much is for sure," Naomi commented.

"And if someone had told me that I would be discussing ancient Chinese philosophy with a young Canadian girl named Naomi—" Chen laughed, and added with twinkling eyes, "My best *tai chi* student."

Naomi chuckled. "Most improved, maybe." She took another sip of tea and thought about what Chen had just said, about destiny and about putting obstacles in one's own path of life. Naomi felt her stomach tighten when she thought about the obstacle she had put in her mother's path. Her hands trembled slightly as she gulped down the last of her tea. The lump in her throat made it hard to swallow.

"Chen," Naomi said. "I think, I did a—bad—thing." Her breath caught.

Chen looked at her with concern. He reached over and put a reassuring hand on the girl's hunched shoulder. No one spoke for several moments.

"This—bad thing you have done. Is there a way you can try to make it right?" Chen asked softly.

Naomi nodded at Chen, then put her head down. She saw tears fall in her lap.

Chen squeezed her shoulder and smiled. "Then you are lucky, Naomi."

Naomi looked up at Chen through her blurry eyes. "But I'm afraid. I'm afraid of things changing and becoming bad. How do you ever know—what your destiny is supposed to be?"

Chen smiled at the girl. "We Chinese know that change is the only thing we can count on in life. We can know nothing of this life, but for the fact that change will occur. Wise people have thus learned to embrace change, and not to fight it." Chen said. He paused thoughtfully for a moment, and grinned. "Remember how we must go with the flow, Naomi. How we must bend and yield, in order to overcome."

Chen took Naomi's hands in his. "Naomi, when people meet, their lives become intertwined—some more than others. Destinies interact. What kind of destiny do you want? Can you accept your fate?" Chen smiled and patted Naomi's hands. "You know—fate can lead us to our destiny—it is a *part* of our destiny. But when we try to avoid it, and take the wrong path, we engage fate in its other meaning, as an *obstacle* in the path to our destiny. When we discover the good way of *thinking* about something, the matter is resolved. The obstacle is overcome and we can move forward. But we must be diligent to keep the correct attitude, or we may lose our way once again."

Naomi nodded, trying to understand everything Chen was telling her.

"Naomi, my child. Go to your destiny. Embrace it. And, above all, do not fear it," Chen said softly, then smiled. "And Naomi, do not forget that you have inherited the Great Dragon's very best qualities."

Naomi listened to Chen in silence, wiping tears from her eyes. Chen rose from his chair and moments later returned with a packet of tissues, and placed it in Naomi's hand. Through her tears, Naomi smiled. She blew her nose and looked up at Chen sheepishly, then reached up and wrapped her arms around the old man. "Thank you, Chen. I love you," Naomi said in a quiet voice. "You are my Chinese grandfather—my family in Hong Kong."

Chen's eye's glistened as he gave Naomi a gentle hug. "And you are my lovely Canadian granddaughter," he replied. "The granddaughter I always wished to have."

At that moment, a gust of wind shook the door and front windows of the shop. Naomi drew back, startled. Chen raised his eyebrows. "Could it be that the typhoon is headed right this way?" He turned to Naomi, and she could see the concern in his eyes. "I think you should go on home, Naomi. Now."

Naomi walked over to the window and looked outside. Rain was beating down on the sidewalk and on the traffic speeding past the shop. The cars and streets gleamed. The sky was dark as if it were already evening, and she could see the thin trees planted along the street bowing deeply in the wind. Naomi smiled. "I think you're right Chen," she said. "It looks like a storm is brewing." Naomi turned to the old man with a look of excitement. "I've never been in a real typhoon before."

Chen looked at her sternly. "A typhoon is a serious thing, Naomi," he replied. "You really must be on your way."

Naomi shrugged, and reluctantly returned to the back of the shop to get her backpack. She didn't want to go home to an empty, lonely apartment. "Okay, Chen, I will," she said. But Naomi was quickly formulating other plans.

Chen handed Naomi an umbrella from the rack nearby and opened the door for her. Naomi smiled at Chen's worried face and said goodbye.

Chen continued to look at Naomi in an uncharacteristically stern manner, "You make sure you go home, Naomi. Hong Kong is not safe in a typhoon. You never know what could happen." But then his face broke out in a grin and he said, "I'll see you in the park tomorrow morning, if the typhoon has passed. Hong Kong is always nice and fresh after a storm."

十九

A strong person faces adversity and remains cheerful despite danger.
This cheerfulness is the source of later success. This stability is stronger
than fate.

—Tao Te Ching

N aomi turned into the wind and headed down the street towards the orphanage. The warm wind and rain were pelting her face as she struggled to open her umbrella. The few other pedestrians Naomi saw seemed to be better prepared for the elements with their slickers and rain ponchos, but they too were struggling to hold onto their own unruly umbrellas. Plumes of water shot out from under passing cars and buses, soaking the legs of the unwary. Naomi stuck close to the buildings as she walked, and she looked up at the sky, awed by the darkness of the clouds. She heard strange creaks and groans and clanking noises, and realized that all of the overhead signs, many of which jutted out over the street on cantilevered supports, were swaying precariously in the wind. Naomi had heard about what could happen in Hong Kong during a typhoon. The dangers were not only sea, but on land as well: falling objects like signs and scattered debris, uprooted trees, landslides, and flash floods. As Naomi turned the corner and headed downhill, a gust of wind turned her umbrella inside-out. Naomi giggled and turned around to right it, realizing it was the first time that this comical occurrence had ever happened to her.

By the time Naomi approached the orphanage, the rain was coming down in a torrent. Ankle-deep water coursed down the street at the curbs, and pooled at the flooded drains. Across the street, Naomi saw a man putting masking tape on his shop front window in a large 'X' shape. Her ears were filled by the howl of wind and the crashing of water on pavement. A huge branch scudded across the street and knocked over a garbage can. *This is serious,* Naomi said to herself, suddenly feeling humbled by the elements wreaking havoc all around her. For a moment Naomi considered taking Chen's advice and heading home, but then decided she'd only get more soaked by waiting for the bus, and that it would be a long time coming, anyway. Besides, she wanted to comfort the children, some of whom would no doubt be afraid of the thunder and lightning. And there was another reason, too. *Grace must be almost ready to have her baby,* Naomi reminded herself as she jogged the last few steps to the orphanage. She opened the door and it shut with a bang behind her, startling the woman behind the desk, who stood up and greeted her with a surprised smile.

"What are you doing here in this weather?" the woman asked.

"It's a long story," Naomi shrugged as she placed her umbrella in the rack by the door and stamped the excess water off herself, letting it drip onto the mat. "Is it okay?"

"Yes, it's okay, I suppose," the woman replied. "But perhaps you should be going home instead. It's a typhoon out there."

"I will, later," Naomi answered cheerfully. She went upstairs to one of the playrooms and peeked in. There they were, her favourite little friends, all turning their heads to see who was at the door.

"Na-mi! Na-mi!" some of them cried, and began running to the door with their arms outstretched. Quickly Naomi opened the door and scampered inside. With a big laugh, Naomi scooped them up in her arms and lay back on the floor, letting the children climb on top of her; on her legs, stomach and head. She forgot all about dragon boats, her mother, Steve, the weather, and focused her attention solely on the children frolicking around her.

Naomi pushed herself up on her elbows and smiled over at the employee who was in the corner changing one of the children. "Excuse me," Naomi said, "Do you know where Grace is?"

The woman carefully placed the girl on the floor and smiled as the child began to crawl towards Naomi. "I think Grace is upstairs in her room," the woman replied.

Naomi continued to play with the children for half an hour, then wondered if she should find Grace. Naomi climbed the stairs and stared down the quiet corridor. All the doors were closed, except for the living room at the top of the stairs, and Naomi wasn't exactly sure which bedroom was Grace's. Naomi tiptoed along the corridor, listening at each door. When she came to the last one on the right, Naomi thought she heard the sound of muffled crying, and knew she had found Grace. Naomi stood at the door for several moments, unsure of what to do. She knocked tentatively and the crying stopped, then Naomi heard Grace say something in Cantonese.

"Grace, it's Naomi," Naomi said.

There was no reply for a long while, and then the door opened. Grace stood before her in a housecoat. She was smiling at Naomi, but her swollen, red-rimmed eyes betrayed the fact that she was upset. "Hello, Naomi," Grace mumbled, trying to put on a cheerful face for her friend.

Naomi looked at Grace gravely. "Is everything okay?" she asked, stepping into the room and closing the door behind her.

Grace nodded. "I'm, well—you know—*I'm pregnant.*" She laughed hollowly, and placed her hands on her protruding belly. She grabbed a tissue from the box by her bed. "I just wish—I just wish—that I could be done with this—*whole thing.*" Naomi could hear Grace getting choked up all over again.

Naomi smiled a small smile. "I figured you must be ready to have your baby soon," Naomi said. The wind was rattling Grace's bedroom window.

"I'm ready," Grace replied. "According to the doctor, I'm even a little overdue—"

Naomi giggled, "Well, just don't have it now—during the typhoon."

Grace nodded sadly and looked down at her round stomach draped in her robe. She attempted a weak smile, but Naomi realized that Grace was ready to cry some more.

Naomi knew that the impending birth was no laughing matter, and she felt ashamed for trying to make light of it. "I'm sorry, Grace. I shouldn't try to be funny—"

"It's okay," Grace mumbled. She looked up at Naomi. "I'll try not to cause problems for anyone—I know the hospitals are always short of staff during a typhoon." Then she tilted her head and asked, "Why are you here, anyway?"

"Well, first I went to see my mom in a dragon boat race. And now she's out partying—"

"In this weather?" Grace asked. "It looks pretty bad out there. I watched the weather report and it said things are going to get worse."

Naomi shrugged. She had to admit that she had no idea where her mother was. "Maybe Mom's gone home. I should give her a call," Naomi said, then added, "But the weather was fine this afternoon, and I decided to come here and visit you—and my friend Chen up the street."

"Thanks, Naomi," Grace said. She clutched Naomi's hand. "I'm glad you came."

There was a knock on the door and the same employee Naomi saw earlier came in with a food tray. She said something to Grace in Cantonese as she placed the tray on Grace's desk.

As the woman left the bedroom, Grace grinned. "She said she gave me extra mango pudding. It's my favourite." Grace surveyed her dinner tray. "Do you want some?"

Naomi shook her head. Her stomach rumbled, and she realized that she was very hungry. "I'm tempted, Grace. But, actually, I think I'd better get going—" She looked out the window.

"Oh please stay a little longer, Naomi. I can't eat all this food. I haven't had much of an appetite today. I've been feeling a little sick all day. Sick and tired. Please stay."

Naomi laughed. "Okay. Okay. I'll stay. And I am hungry. You'll have to give me some of your mango pudding, though."

Grace grinned. "No problem," she said, and sat down at the small desk while Naomi pulled up another chair and sat next to her. Shoulder to shoulder, they two girls ate in silence. From time to time, they looked out the window at the storm. It was dark now, but the street lights illuminated the rain that was pelting down in noisy gusts. Suddenly, someone was knocking at the door and the girls could hear it open before they had a chance to turn around.

"What are you doing here?"

Naomi saw a soaked Edith standing in the doorway. She looked upset. "I was told you were here," Edith said in exasperation. "What on earth are you doing here during a typhoon?" Water was dripping off her hair and down her face. She didn't seem to notice.

"I just stopped by, to play with the kids. And I thought I'd come up and see how Grace was doing—"

Edith's face softened a little. "That's nice of you, Naomi," she said. But then her expression became serious once again and she pointed to the window. "But can't you see we are in the middle of a typhoon?"

Naomi suddenly felt foolish. "I'm sorry," she said meekly. "This is my first typhoon. I guess I didn't realize that it's such a big deal. I wasn't going to stay for very long—everyone has been telling me to go home. I guess I should have listened." Naomi looked nervously at her watch. *Where has the time gone?* It was almost eight o'clock. Naomi looked apologetically at Grace, then at Edith, and stood up. "I was just going to leave."

Edith put her hands on her hips and shook her head. "I can't let you go out in this weather. There's a Signal Eight typhoon raging out there, Naomi. You're not going anywhere now."

Naomi gulped. "Signal Eight?" She glanced over at Grace and thought she detected the traces of a smile cross the girl's lips.

"Well, it's not like we don't have room for you. There's an empty room next door. You can sleep there tonight," Edith said. After a pause, she added. "Actually, I need your help. The overnight staff will not be coming in. You will earn your keep tonight, Naomi." She glanced at the tray on the desk and laughed. "Call your mother, and—goodness, Naomi, come downstairs and get some of your own food. Grace needs to eat all her food—by herself."

❦   ❦

"Naomi, I'm glad you're here," Grace said. "Thanks for staying in my room with me. I'm sorry you have to sleep on the floor, though. But thank you."

Naomi sat up on one elbow and looked up at Grace. Naomi could see the outline of Grace's head as the girl looked down from her bed. She could tell how much it meant to Grace that she was not alone. "That's okay. I like sleeping on the floor. It reminds me of camping," she replied, then giggled. "I'm just glad I don't have to camp in the rain."

Grace laughed. It was a small and sad little laugh. Naomi could tell that Grace was afraid. *I'm glad it's not me,* Naomi admitted to herself. *I'm so glad that it's not me.* She reached up and took a hold of Grace's hand in the darkness. "Don't be afraid, Grace," Naomi whispered. "Everything is going to be all right."

"Thank you, Naomi," Grace replied. Her voice wavered.

Naomi gave Grace's hand a reassuring squeeze and lay back down on the floor. The two girls listened in silence to the thunderbolts and pelting rain. There were other noises, too, and neither Naomi nor Grace could guess what was happening out there in the streets of Hong Kong, in the typhoon. The storm was getting stronger, and moving closer to Hong Kong. Naomi realized she was feeling a little afraid, too, and wasn't sure if it was due to the typhoon, or because of thoughts of Grace and childbirth.

Although Naomi had never thought about it much, childbirth was something that she found both awesome and frightening. Sara had told Naomi about her own birth; how Naomi's head had been in a breech position, making the contractions very painful. Initially, Sara had wanted to have a natural delivery with no anaesthetic drugs, but as the contractions started to become so painful, and the doctors realized the situation, Sara was offered an epidural—a special pain-killing injection in the spinal cord. And then the epidural hadn't worked! Sara said there wasn't a lot that could be done at that point, and that she was glad that Naomi's father was there to hold her hand. 'But I would do it all over again—just to have you,' Sara had said every time she told this story. It was, after all, as Baba liked to say, 'water under the bridge'. Still, Naomi felt frightened for Grace. She lay on the mattress, turning from side to side, hoping to get comfortable, and could tell that Grace was also having a sleepless night up on her bed. It was quite some time before Naomi finally fell asleep—

"Naomi. Are you awake?—NAOMI? Are you AWAKE?"

Naomi awoke with a start, and realized that Grace was hitting the side of her bed with her palm, trying to get Naomi's attention. She sat up and looked at her friend, who was laying in bed, crying. A sense of foreboding enveloped Naomi.

"Grace!" she cried out.

"Something's happening!"

二十

Life is a dream upon waking...

"I'm sorry," Grace stammered. "I think—something's happening."

"What do you mean something's happening?" Naomi asked incredulously. She looked at her watch. It was 4:18 in the morning.

"I'm—I'm not feeling very good—"

"You're having your baby? Are you having your baby? NOW?"

Grace winced. Naomi looked at her own hand and realized that she was gripping Grace's arm tightly. She let go.

"I—don't—know!" Grace replied, and muffled a sob.

Naomi stood up. *I wouldn't have a clue what being in labour feels like, either,* she said to herself as she hurried to the light switch on the wall. "Wait here. I'm going to find someone." Naomi began pulling on her shorts.

Grace nodded forlornly from the bed. Naomi opened the bedroom door and ran down the stairs as quietly as she could. Outside, the typhoon was raging. Naomi made her way to the front desk area, which was deserted, and then pushed open the door to Edith's office. Edith was asleep on the sofa next to her desk, and a book was on the floor next to her. The light was on.

"Edith!" said Naomi, breathless.

Edith sat up. "Is it Grace?"

Naomi nodded and Edith rose from the sofa. Naomi thought she was moving a little too slowly and calmly. "Well, then. It's about time. It appears that Grace's baby is not going to wait out any Signal Eight typhoon."

"Is it really true?" Naomi asked as they made their way upstairs.

Edith turned to Naomi and smiled. "It had to happen sooner or later." As they climbed the stairs, Edith whispered, "I always get excited when it's time. Grace will be frightened right now—but we will help her." She stopped half-way up the stairs and put her hand on Naomi's arm. "I am going to need your help, Naomi. You and I will take Grace to the hospital, but I will have to come back. Okay?"

Naomi nodded. Dread and adrenaline coursed through her body. They neared Grace's room and Edith squeezed Naomi's arm reassuringly as they entered. "How do you feel, Grace?" Edith asked as she sat down on the bed next to the girl.

Grace put her hand across her lower abdomen. "It's feels strange here. Tight. It hurts. It's been going on for quite some time—"

"How long?" Edith asked gently.

Grace thought for a moment. "For a few hours. Since before we went to bed—but only a few times, at the beginning," she added hastily.

Now Naomi could see the growing alarm in Edith's face. "You felt a pain only a few times before. But now—how often do you feel them now?" Edith asked.

"A lot now." Grace clenched her teeth and shut her eyes. Naomi could hear the girl sucking in her breath. She clutched at the bed sheets. "Now!" Grace cried out through clenched teeth. She threw her head back and groaned.

"Grace. Squeeze my hand. You are having a contraction. Apparently you've been having them for quite a while. You should have said something earlier on, when they were starting. We talked about all this before, don't you remember?" Edith said, then shook her head. "Never mind. Are the contractions coming about every ten minutes?"

"No. More than that," Grace burst into sobs. "I'm sorry. I waited too long—"

Edith rose and began to help Grace from the bed. Without looking at Naomi, she said, "Grace's suitcase is in the closet. It's already packed. Go wake up Mrs. Lai in the staff bedroom. Tell her to call a taxi. Take the suitcase down to the front door and then come back here."

Naomi grabbed the suitcase, then went to the staff bedroom at the end of the hall and knocked on the door. Within seconds, Mrs. Lai was at the door, looking dishevelled and sleepy.

"Grace needs a taxi to the hospital," Naomi said breathlessly.

The old woman nodded. "I'll call one. But with this weather, I hope it's not urgent."

Panic swept over Naomi. "It is urgent—I think," she said. She watched Mrs. Lai pick up the phone next to her bed, then ran down the stairs, depositing the suitcase by the front door. When Naomi returned upstairs she met Grace and Edith on the top stairway, and watched anxiously as Grace made her way down, holding onto Edith and the banister for support. In the stairwell, illuminated only by small night light, Naomi could see the fear in Grace's face. "Don't be afraid, Grace. Everything is going to be okay," Naomi said again, trying to sound reassuring. But her own voice was quavering, and Naomi's stomach sank when Grace began to sob again as they reached the lobby. Mrs. Lai came down behind them.

"No taxi," Mrs. Lai said gravely.

Edith nodded. She went to the front door and looked down the street for a moment. When she looked back at the others, her face was already dripping with rain. She smiled at Grace. "It's only three blocks. We have to go now. You can do it, Grace."

Mrs. Lai went into the office and emerged with three umbrellas. "We'll only be needing one," Edith said, and took the biggest one from Mrs. Lai. She turned to Naomi and Grace. "We'll walk close together, like in a sack race. Naomi and I will hold you up when you get a contraction, Grace. Hopefully you will get only one or two on the way." She stepped through the door and opened the umbrella. "Mrs. Lai, call the hospital and tell them we will be arriving on foot at their south entrance in about ten minutes. Okay, girls. Let's go."

The three huddled close, with Grace in the middle. They hadn't gone ten steps when Naomi felt Grace's legs buckle. Naomi steadied herself and held on tight to her friend.

"Breathe, Grace. Take a deep breath. Concentrate on that," Edith said encouragingly.

Naomi struggled to hold up Grace, who was barely standing on her own feet by now. The girl's strange groans frightened Naomi. After several seconds, Grace was able to stand up again and she took a deep breath. "Okay," the girl whispered hoarsely.

They crossed one street and a fresh gust of wind whipped rain under the meagre protection of the umbrella. Soon they were all soaked. "Two blocks to go," Edith said, and then, "Grace, try to make it to the end of the block before you have your next contraction."

Two blocks down, Naomi said to herself. There was no traffic on the streets and they didn't wait for the crossing signal to change to green. Through the pelting rain, Naomi could see the entrance to the hospital. *Almost there!* She began to pick up her pace but was held back by Grace, who suddenly stopped, her face twisted in agony. Again, Grace's legs buckled, and Naomi struggled to hold onto the pregnant girl, as the rain continued to drench them all.

"Someone's coming," Edith yelled, and Naomi looked up to see a hospital orderly running towards them. Edith, Grace and the orderly exchanged words in Cantonese. Naomi moved out of the way so he could grab Grace. Edith thrust her chin at Naomi as she spoke to the orderly and Naomi could see him glancing at her before he replied. Naomi wished she could understand what was being said. As they climbed the stairs to the hospital, Naomi breathed a sigh of relief.

"You did a good job, Naomi," Edith said as they headed up to the first floor, which housed the labour and maternity wards.

Naomi took a seat in the small waiting area. All of a sudden she felt very tired. She looked at her legs and watched the water drip down, forming rivulets that made puddles at her feet. *Everything's going to be okay—*

Edith walked over to Naomi, taking the seat beside her. She put a hand on Naomi's damp shoulder and smiled. "Grace is fine. The doctors are examining her now and she will be assigned to a bed in the labour ward. She may not be there for long, from what I can tell. They may be moving her to the delivery room within the hour." She looked intently at Naomi. "Thanks for being here—for Grace." Edith pushed some strands of wet hair from her forehead. "Grace is going to need you now. Will you go up and stay with her in the labour ward? Normally, visitors aren't allowed at this time of the night, but I have explained the circumstances and they have agreed, although reluctantly."

Naomi gulped and nodded, and before she had a chance to speak, Edith spoke again. "Thank you, Naomi, for doing this. I would of course be here myself, but I don't know how long this is going to take and soon the children will start to wake up. Mrs. Lai can't manage on her own. I must go back. We are short-staffed."

Naomi nodded again, and followed Edith to the labour ward. Grace was laying in a big bed, wearing a pink hospital gown. Around her arm was a band of wires that were connected to a machine on a trolley next to her. *She looks so small and scared in that big bed,* Naomi thought to herself, and was glad to see how Grace's face visibly brightened when she saw her entering the ward, which was empty but for Grace.

"Stay with me, Naomi?" Grace asked.

"Yes," Naomi replied.

Grace and Edith spoke in Cantonese. Grace nodded and Edith bent down to give her a kiss on the cheek. She turned to Naomi. "Take care of Grace," she said, then bent closer to Naomi and whispered, "The staff here are strict about rules. They have told me they don't want you to go into the delivery room. You aren't her family. But, Naomi, I am asking you, if you think you can handle it, try to get in there with Grace. She shouldn't be alone. I have asked them to make an exception under this situation, but I don't have to time to argue with them. I must go back now."

Naomi nodded, nervousness coursing through her body. She watched Edith leave and then turned to Grace, who was looking at her forlornly. Naomi looked at her watch. It was almost six o'clock in the morning.

Grace smiled wanly. "There's a waiting room with a TV over there— if you don't want to sit with me. It's where the husbands wait, I guess."

Naomi giggled, buoyed by Grace's attempt at humour. A nurse walked over to check Grace's monitor and smiled at the two girls. "There's a drink machine in the waiting room. But I'm afraid the cafeteria won't be open for another hour," she said.

"That's okay," Naomi replied. She took a seat next to Grace's bed and watched as a nurse monitored Grace's contractions. It didn't take long for Naomi to figure out that the numbers on the monitor rose whenever Grace began another contraction. Now, by looking at the monitor, Naomi could see that another contraction was imminent. Naomi grabbed Grace's hand as the contraction took hold of her. Naomi could only watch, helpless and confused, as the girl's body was seemingly wracked by something that was not a part of her. The number on the monitor had shot up to 150, where it hovered for several moments, and then fell back down once again. Naomi watched Grace exhale deeply and she did the same. Another contraction was over.

Just after 7:30, a doctor came in and examined Grace. "It's time to move you into the delivery room," he announced matter-of-factly. Two midwives appeared and lifted some levers on Grace's bed, making it instantly mobile. Naomi watched as Grace was wheeled down the corridor along with the monitor. Timidly she followed behind the group, not sure what to do next, but knowing that she needed to stick close to her friend.

A nurse stationed at the doorway of the labour ward said, "I'm sorry, but you'll have to stay in the waiting room. Only relatives—"

"NAAAAOMIIIIIIII!" Grace wailed. "COME WITH ME! PLEASE!"

Naomi remembered what Edith had told her. Grace was all alone. *I need to be with Grace.* Naomi told herself. She knew she needed to assert herself here, and she faced the nurse squarely. "I know that Edith has explained the situation to you. Under the circumstances, it's important that Grace is not alone in there. I have been instructed to stay with her." Naomi held her breath.

The nurse glowered at Naomi for a moment, then stood up. "All right. I'll get you something to wear in the delivery room. The woman returned moments later and handed Naomi a long-sleeved pink shirt and something that looked like a big white shower cap.

"Put these on and follow me," the nurse said and headed to the delivery room. As Naomi entered, a kind-looking midwife smiled at her and led her over to Grace. She handed Naomi a cool washcloth and said,

"Having a baby is hard work. You can wipe Grace's forehead. That's your job." They both looked over at Grace as another contraction bore into her. "Let her hold onto your hand," the midwife said to Naomi.

Naomi took her place, standing next to Grace's head. "You can do it," Naomi whispered to Grace. "Squeeze my hand."

Grace grabbed Naomi's arm at the wrist and began digging her fingernails deeply into Naomi's skin. Naomi winced. "Uh, Grace. Not quite so hard—"

"S-sorry," Grace whispered, and let go. Moments later Naomi could feel Grace's grip tighten once again.

"Push. Push," the two midwives urged Grace. Grace bore down, straining, and she soon collapsed back on the bed. "Good girl!" the midwives cried and began to applaud. Naomi could see Grace smiling. Another contraction; more praise and applause from the midwives, and another proud smile from Grace. Naomi wiped Grace's forehead dutifully, not quite believing the strange scenario that she found herself involved in.

"The baby's head is crowning," one of the midwives said. Suddenly a doctor appeared, and he examined Grace and the baby, whose birth was imminent. Grace lay in bed, breathing heavily, exhausted. Naomi looked at the monitor, the numbers were rising again, and she knew that Grace would soon be going through another contraction. Naomi smiled at Grace as the girl clenched her arm in a vice-like grip.

"Push, Grace. One more big push," the midwife said.

Grace pushed as hard as she could through the contraction and her body shook with the effort. She cried out in pain and exhaustion. Naomi held her breath, oblivious to Grace's grip, and watched as the baby's head emerged from between Grace's legs. There were no words. Naomi looked at the midwives who seemed calm and completely at ease. One smiled up at Grace and clapped her hands again. "Good girl." She then spoke in Cantonese and Grace nodded. Grace's body was preparing for another contraction. Naomi could see Grace's face begin to twist into pain once more. And before Naomi really understood what was happening, the rest of the baby's body emerged along with a flood of fluids and blood. A low moan emerged from Grace's lips. One midwife was clapping as the other bundled the baby in towels, and Naomi found herself clapping too.

The midwife spoke to Grace, "Your baby is being washed and examined now. But we'll bring it right back. And you will discover what your baby is."

At that moment, the other midwife returned to Grace with the baby bundled neatly in a towel. She held the bundle in front of Grace. "You must tell us what sex your baby is. Lift the blanket and tell us."

A bit dazed, Grace did as she was told. She lifted the blanket and looked at her baby's red, naked body. "It's a boy!" Grace cried out. Her face crumpled into a sob. Naomi put her hand on Grace's shoulder, not knowing what to say, but tried to imagine what Grace was feeling at that moment.

"The baby is healthy," the midwife said, and laid the bundle in Grace's arms. Grace's body shook with sobs as she held her baby. For a moment no one spoke, then Grace shook her head and slowly returned the baby to the midwife. After a final examination, an orderly came in to take Grace to the maternity ward.

"Thank you, Naomi," Grace said simply as she was wheeled away in her bed. Naomi could see her shoulders heaving with silent sobs.

Naomi followed the bed out of the delivery room and watched as the orderly pushed the bed down the corridor. Naomi stood motionless, her mind a jumble of awe and sorrow and confusion. *What is she thinking?* Naomi wondered. She wanted to follow Grace, but her feet felt glued to the floor.

The delivering midwife joined Naomi in the corridor and put a hand on her shoulder. "It was good that you were here." The woman led Naomi to a chair, then patted her hand and was off.

Naomi didn't know what was going to happen next. She felt strangely empty inside. Slowly, as if emerging from a trance, Naomi realized it was time to head home. Her job at the hospital was over. On the way out of the hospital, Naomi stopped to peek in the doorway of the maternity ward, where the newborn babies were kept. There were two tiny babies inside. Both were sleeping in their bassinets, bundled up in their blue and white striped hospital-issue flannels. Naomi stared in awe at Grace's baby boy, his head covered with a thick thatch of black hair. The baby yawned. Naomi smiled, and a surge of pride swept through her. *I was there the moment you were born,* Naomi spoke silently to the boy. *And it was a miracle.*

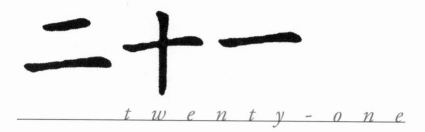

...death is a going home.

—Chinese Proverb

N aomi skipped down the front stairs of the hospital, and noticed that Hong Kong had become a different place overnight. The sun was already high and shining in a cloudless sky. The air seemed vivid and alive and smelled fresh. Naomi looked up and down the street and saw that it was strewn with debris; mostly tree branches and leaves. All of a sudden Naomi felt full of energy. *What had just happened?* It was the most unforgettable day she had ever experienced. Naomi began to jog to the bus stop but then stopped. *I'll die if I can't tell someone now,* she thought to herself. With a grin, she turned and headed towards Hollywood Road, and Chen.

Naomi noticed that most of the shopkeepers were out on the street already, cleaning up in front of their shops after the typhoon. Some were sweeping leaves into small piles, while others were sluicing down their parts of the sidewalk, which had been covered in grime from the rain. A few shopkeepers were busy scraping remnants of masking tape from their windows. As Naomi approached Chen's shop, she was surprised to see that he was not out in front like everyone else, cleaning away the aftermath of the storm. She pulled at the door. It was locked. Naomi peered in the window, but the shop was darkened and there was no movement inside. She frowned. *Chen was never late, he'd said.*

"I guess it'll have to wait," Naomi said with a shrug, and sprinted to the bus stop just as a bus pulled up. As the bus made its way to Happy Valley, Naomi saw city clean-up crews busy sweeping curbs free of the collected debris. One street had been blocked off and two fire engines were parked nearby. Naomi craned her neck as the bus passed the side street, and gasped. An entire wall of bamboo scaffolding had come loose from a building that had been under renovation. The top portion of the scaffolding lay in a crumpled heap in the narrow street. Naomi could make out the bright colours of the vehicles that had been parked in the street and were now buried under tonnes of bamboo.

When the bus finally came to her stop, Naomi almost jumped off. She ran into her building and slammed the elevator button, watching with impatience as the numbers lit up down to zero. By the time she arrived at the front door she thought she was going to burst. Naomi couldn't wait to tell her mother about her adventure, about Grace and the baby. In her impatience she tried the door and found, to her surprise, that it was unlocked. "Mom! Guess what!" she yelled out as she burst in the door, then abruptly stopped. Sitting at the dining-table was her mother. Steve was standing next to her, with his hand on her shoulder. Both of them looked up at Naomi, startled at her sudden entrance. Naomi stared into their faces, and the triumphant smile was wiped from her lips. Naomi realized that her mother and Steve were both staring at her with stricken faces. No one spoke. Finally, Naomi took a step forward and dropped her backpack. Her eyes were wide with fear.

"What happened?" Naomi whispered, almost too afraid to ask.

Naomi watched her mother's eyes fill with tears as she rose out of the chair. She reached her arms out to Naomi. "Oh, Naomi," she said softly. "It's Chen. Chen is dead." She wrapped her arms around her daughter.

Naomi felt like the breath had been sucked out of her. She couldn't speak. She couldn't believe the words her mother had just spoken. *It's not true. It's not true!* her mind screamed. Still in her mother's embrace, Naomi looked over her mother's shoulder at Steve, who was looking at her with tears in his own eyes. Naomi opened her mouth, but nothing came out. And then, finally, she whispered, "No."

Naomi could feel her mother's arms hold her even more tightly, and she felt her mother nodding. "Yes. It was on the news this morning." Sara pulled back to face her daughter, grabbing both her arms. "They say he's missing, presumed drowned." Tears rolled down her cheeks. "He saved two boys—"

"OH NO! OH NO!" Naomi wailed. She felt her legs go weak. Steve came over and grabbed her arm. Together, Sara and Steve led Naomi over to the sofa. Naomi bent forward and wept.

Chen's body was found floating in the harbour two days later. In the days that followed the typhoon, the heroic last act of Chen Ying Kwong was told to Hong Kong in the newspapers and on television. The two little boys, who admitted to playing frequently in the drainage ditch, told of how they had been trying to walk across a log that had lodged among the debris and how they had fallen off, but remained clutching the log and screaming for help. Several minutes later their hero had appeared and climbed down into the flooded ditch. He reached across and grabbed the hand of one boy, pulling him to safety. As the water continued to rage, Chen did not hesitate to enter the torrent to retrieve the second boy. As the first boy explained, it had appeared that, as Chen reached for the boy, the log he had been standing on began to dislodge from the rest of the collected debris. Chen grabbed the boy and threw him into the pile of branches on the opposite side of the ditch. The two boys then watched in horror as Chen fell into the water and was swept away.

Naomi lay on the sofa in her apartment, her red-rimmed eyes watching another newscast, listening to the story of her friend's heroic death once again. She had barely slept in three days. But her ears pricked up at some new information being spoken by the news announcer: "Chen Ying Kwong was predeceased by his wife and son in 1968." Naomi sat up, and suddenly felt sick.

Two days later, Naomi and her mother attended a memorial service for Chen. As she sat stiffly in her chair, willing herself not to cry, Naomi noticed that the memorial hall was full and well-attended by the news media. Naomi looked around the room and saw all of Chen's *tai chi* friends. A Buddhist monk spoke for a while, and also someone who Naomi suspected was a civil servant of some kind, but it was all in Cantonese and she didn't know what they were saying. Naomi sat through the service thinking her own thoughts about Chen; a friend, a teacher, a mentor. Naomi watched absently as another man walked forward and began to speak. Slowly Naomi was drawn out of her private reverie. The voice sounded familiar. Naomi scrutinized the man at the podium and the realization hit her; *He's Chen's brother.* Naomi felt certain of it. As the service ended and people began to file out, Naomi's eyes remained fixed on the man as he was approached by several members of Chen's *tai chi* group as well as others who wanted to offer their condolences. Naomi longed to go over and talk to him, but she had no idea what to say—or if he would even be able to understand her. Without a word, she followed her mother out into street.

The next day, Naomi got up early as usual and headed to the coffee shop. Her eyes brimmed over with tears as she passed the park, a place of many happy memories but now strangely empty. At the coffee shop, Naomi ordered a latte and grabbed a paper off the rack, instantly noticing the front page photo of a rather stern-looking Chen. The headline read: *Typhoon Hero to Receive Posthumous Bravery Award.* Naomi blinked back tears, trying to bring the letters into focus: *Chen Ying Kwong will be given posthumously the Gold Medal of Bravery, says a spokeswoman from the Office of the Chief Executive—*

Naomi dabbed her eyes with her napkin and smiled. She felt proud to be a friend of a man who was going to receive such an honour, but knew that the honour was not something her friend would have been as excited about. It was not his style. *Chen was an unassuming man,* Naomi thought. *He saved those boys because he cared about them so much. If he was alive, Chen would probably laugh at all this attention—or wave it off.* Naomi almost giggled through her tears at the thought, but as quickly as it came the thought was overcome by a wave of devastation and loss. Her arm shook as she took a swallow of tea, and Naomi took a few deep breaths trying to dissolve the lump in her throat and calm herself down. And then, at that moment, a voice from inside her told her to go to Chen's shop. Without stopping to ponder this, Naomi rose from the table and a cab appeared as she stepped into the street. "Hollywood Road," she instructed the driver.

The taxi let her off in front of Chen's shop, and Naomi pulled on the door, which was locked. Naomi peered in the window. The place was deserted. Just as Naomi turned to leave, the man she had seen at the memorial service emerged from the back room. Naomi banged on the door. The man looked up and came towards the door. Naomi looked at the man, a stranger, yet familiar all at once.

"I—I," Naomi croaked as the man stood in the open doorway.

The man smiled gently, and his eyes sparkled like Chen's. Naomi felt it was as if Chen's eyes were peering at her through another man's face. "I know who you are," the man said simply. Naomi realized that his English was refined like Chen's, although his accent was a little stronger. "I'm glad that you came. Please come in."

Naomi followed the man to the back of the shop. He motioned for her to sit down and began to pour some tea. With a small bow she took the cup that the man handed her, and remembered that she had played out this simple scenario with Chen countless times before.

"I know who you are, Naomi. Do you know who I am?" asked the man with a smile as he sat down next to her.

Naomi nodded. "You're Chen's brother. From China. He told me about you."

The man nodded. "My brother told me about you, too. He wrote me letters about the lovely Canadian young lady who was learning *tai chi*." He sipped his tea and continued. "He cared very much about you." Naomi could see the man's expression darken slightly. "He cared very much about how you were doing—adjusting to Hong Kong and the other new things happening in your life."

Naomi nodded.

"I want you to know that you were a special person to my brother. He considered you like a granddaughter. He told me this," Chen's brother continued. "I would like to thank you for giving him this special gift. It was very important to him—"

"Chen was important to me, too," Naomi blurted out, wiping away a tear. She looked from her teacup to Chen's brother and held her breath. Finally, she spoke. There was something she needed to know—something she had wondered about and yet feared. "Chen never told me he had a family," she began.

The man put his teacup on the table and rested his hands on his knees. For a long time he didn't speak. Finally, he looked up at Naomi and pursed his lips, nodding. "I wonder if I am to tell you—since my brother didn't tell you himself. But I think we have met for a reason. Maybe he wanted you to know, after all."

Tears sprang to Naomi's eyes and she wiped them away with the back of her hand.

"I am sure my brother told you about how he came to Hong Kong," Chen's brother began.

"He said that he came here during the Cultural Revolution in China," Naomi answered, nodding.

The man looked at Naomi, as if waiting to hear more. He smiled. "My brother never told you the circumstances of his arrival in Hong Kong?"

Naomi shook her head.

"Well. It is a long story. Have some more hot tea," Chen's brother said as he filled Naomi's cup. "In China, in 1968, society was in chaos. The Cultural Revolution had been instigated and everyone lived in fear— particularly people who had associations with so-called 'Western influences'. Our father was not only a university professor, but he had a close association with Westerners living in our city. We all waited for the day that he, and perhaps even our mother, would be sent to a labour camp to be, as the Communists put it, 're-educated' and 're-habilitated'.

"My brother was 24 years old at the time, and he had been married only two years. He had a baby boy. That was when the persecution of my father started. My father was forced to attend nightly neighbourhood meetings where he, and others like him, were forced to write long essays admitting to being all sorts of evil things: 'the running dog of Western imperialism', 'capitalist-roader', 'class enemy'. Oh, the things they thought of," Chen's brother said with a sad smile.

"Soon after he was forced to publicly admit his guilt, he was subjected to a public humiliation in what were called 'struggle meetings'. All the adults in our neighbourhood were forced to attend, including my mother and brother. At these meetings, the people would shout insults and accusations at my father. They would throw things, like eggs and tomatoes, at him. Of course, my mother and brother kept silent at these meetings, refusing to go along with the crowd. But then, one day, the neighbourhood council told my brother that he would be expected to *lead* the struggle meetings against my father. That was when my brother told me he was going to try to make it to Hong Kong. He had been thinking about trying it for a while, simply because he wanted to find a better life for us all in Hong Kong, but now he had become desperate to leave. There was no way that he was going to denounce our father. He would've rather died."

Chen's brother took a sip of his tea, and continued. "My brother gave me all his savings, to take care of his wife while he was gone. I was simply to tell her not to worry and that he would find a way to send for her and their son, and perhaps even the rest of us. The plan was that he would pay a smuggler to take him to Hong Kong by boat. These smugglers are called 'snakeheads'. He left our town on some pretext—I don't remember what exactly—and then he headed for the coast. He secured a place on a boat run by these snakeheads and was soon on his way to Hong Kong. There was a storm that night. The boat capsized as it was nearing Hong Kong. Several of the stowaways drowned, my brother later told me. Others were picked up by Chinese patrol boats. And as for my brother—he, of course, made it to safety. Perhaps he was the only one. I don't know. He was a strong swimmer, and he swam to shore. How fortunate for him that he had washed up on Hong Kong soil. Back then, Hong Kong's policy was that any mainlander who reached Hong Kong soil would be granted the right of abode by the British Government. It is one of the many ironies of my brother's life."

Chen's brother took a deep breath, then continued. "He made it to Hong Kong. And, knowing my brother, he wasted no time in getting himself settled here and earning a living so that he could one day be reunited with his wife and son. But what happened—" the man shook his head. "Those that survived the capsize were sent back in disgrace, to prison in their towns. And since my brother's body was never found, those that had met him on that perilous journey began to talk. Word got back to our town that my brother had been on a boat with other people attempting to leave China, and that he had drowned. We were devastated. Weeks later, the town council swooped in on my family again. But this time they had a fresh reason to persecute my father at the struggle meetings. They accused my father of trying to convince his son to leave Hong Kong—to be a traitor to his country.

"One day, a band of young thugs—the Red Guard—broke into our home." Chen's brother put his head in his hands before looking up again, blinking away tears. "They threatened us, and some of them took my parents off to the police station for more intimidation. I, of course, followed them. My sister-in-law, who was living with us, was still at our home with her son. While I was gone, the Red Guard began to ransack our home. They piled all our books and paintings in the middle of the room, and lit them on fire. To everyone's horror, the fire began to quickly burn out of control and they dragged my sister-in-law into the street. One thug punched my sister-in-law, who was screaming hysterically, and she fell unconscious." Chen's brother was crying freely by now, and he reached for a tissue. "My sister-in-law had hidden my nephew in a cupboard, worried that the Red Guard would harm the baby or try to take him away from us. The house was burned to the ground."

Naomi's eyes filled with tears and she began to sob silently.

"—my sister-in-law killed herself one month later."

Neither Naomi nor Chen's brother spoke for several moments.

"When my brother got word to me from Hong Kong a year later, I couldn't believe it. I thought he was dead, like the rumours had said. In fact, all that time, I had been grateful for this knowledge—he would never know the fate of his wife and son. My brother told me he was going to pay some snakeheads to bring his wife and son to Hong Kong, and that eventually he would bring us all over to Hong Kong. He wanted to know how everyone was, especially, of course, his wife and son. It was the worst day of my life—the day I had to tell him that they had been killed by the Red Guard. It was only much later that I told him the whole truth."

Naomi stared at the man next to her, barely able to breathe, not wanting to believe the tragedy that she had just been told. The truth of Chen's past was unbearable. And the fact that he would die such a tragic death himself seemed so unfair. Naomi put her head in her arms and continued to sob. She thought she was hearing things when she heard Chen's brother chuckle softly. "My brother was always a excellent swimmer. Why else would he be so foolish to go out and try to rescue someone from drowning during a typhoon. He forgot he was an old man."

Naomi looked up at the man. He was smiling. "I'm proud of my brother," he said. "It doesn't surprise me at all that he met the end of his time on earth by helping two young boys to live. No, it doesn't surprise me at all." Chen's brother slapped his knee. "There's something I want to do—before I start to pack up my brother's personal items."

"What will you do with the shop?" Naomi asked.

"I'll sell it. My brother was a noble, responsible man. He blamed himself for his wife and son's deaths. But he will be pleased to know that his little business here will put his brother's granddaughter through university."

Naomi followed Chen's brother to the front room, and watched him take a photo from his briefcase. It was the photo of Chen that she had seen in the newspaper. Chen's brother placed it front of the altar on the shelf, next to the two other photos: the one of two unsmiling people—his mother and father; and the other one, faded and torn and well-worn, which Naomi now knew was a photo of Chen's young wife and their little boy.

Chen's brother lit some incense sticks and said, "We Chinese have a saying. That life is like a dream. Because once you have woken up from a dream, only then do you realize that the beauty of what you saw was actually your life." Chen's brother paused. "We also believe that dying is simply a return to ourselves—to our home. My brother is home now." They stood in silence for several moments, looking at the three photos. Then the man cleared his throat and began to put some items from behind the counter into a box.

"Let me help you," Naomi said. She looked under the counter and began bringing piles of papers onto the countertop. She had no idea what the papers were, her eyes were blurred by tears. She simply wanted to do something, to help.

Chen's brother came over and put his hand on Naomi's arm. "It's okay."

Naomi nodded, and knew that he was expecting her to leave. But she wanted to stay. Naomi knew that once she left the shop she would be out of Chen's life forever. Naomi looked one last time around the shop. She took a deep breath. "I am glad to have met you," she said.

"And I am very pleased to have met you, Naomi," Chen's brother replied. He patted Naomi on the shoulder, then turned and walked over to some shelves. He removed an object from one of the shelves and placed it in Naomi's hands. "I want you to have something, Naomi. My brother told me you are on a journey." His eyes twinkled, just like Chen's did. "I hope this little friend will help you find your way."

Naomi looked down at the object in her hands. It was small, perfect, bronze rabbit.

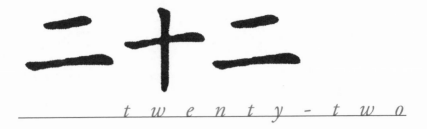

twenty - two

If I hold a green bough in my heart—a singing bird will come.

—Chinese Proverb

From time to time over the next year, Naomi and her mother or her friends would find an excuse to go for a walk down Hollywood Road, but Naomi could never enjoy it as much as she used to. A few days after Naomi's meeting with Chen's brother, the shop was sold. For months, the front windows of the little shop had been covered in white paint and later that year an Indian restaurant opened up in its place.

Naomi never saw Grace again after her boy was born on the night of the typhoon, but the child was a special new addition among the residents at Mother's Love. Naomi and her mother doted on the child, and Naomi continued to make weekly visits to the orphanage, hoping that Grace would come by, but she never did. Once, Naomi asked Edith if she could have Grace's telephone number, but this was against policy, and Edith would not give it to her. Naomi often wondered how Grace was doing; if she would be going back to school—or perhaps back to a job—and whether she was reconciled with her family.

One day, when Naomi went to the orphanage as usual, she was devastated to discover that Grace's little boy was gone. He had been adopted by a family from Hong Kong. Now she knew for herself about that ache in her heart—the one that Edith had warned her about—when volunteers become so attached to the youngsters in their care. Naomi

146

often wondered about the boy's new family, and how he was being taken care of. She swore she would never forget the little boy's face, and the moment that he came into the world.

School brought a welcome, familiar routine back into Naomi's life, something to help Naomi take her mind off the new world around her. Once again, she met everyday with Jovita and her other chattering friends. But something had changed for Naomi. She no longer had the same interest in discussing pop stars and shopping bargains. Life now seemed a little more complicated and mysterious.

Every morning, Naomi chose to walk to the bus stop up the street from her apartment block, instead of the one down near the coffee shop, in order to avoid looking into the small park, which was empty and silent.

The autumn wind blew briskly across a clear blue sky. From the top of the mountain, Naomi looked out over the hills in the east, past the skyscrapers along the border into China, in the direction of Chen's home. She remembered a Chinese proverb that she had found in a book her mother had given her: *Worry not that no one knows of you; seek to be worth knowing.*

"You were worth knowing, Chen," Naomi whispered. "You will be in my heart and in my mind—always."

"Oof."

Naomi smiled when she heard that familiar masculine voice. And then she heard her mother's laughter.

"I think she wants down," Sara said.

Naomi turned around and grinned. "I'll take her, Dad," she said to Steve, and reached for the wiggling girl sitting atop the man's shoulders. The little girl wrapped her arms around Naomi eagerly.

"I love you Mei-mei," Naomi whispered in her ear. The little girl put her hands on Naomi's head and her lips on Naomi's cheek. Naomi squeezed her tightly and looked over to the two people who were smiling down at her. At that moment, a realization burned bright in Naomi's mind: *My destiny—is standing right in front of me.* Naomi could see it reflected back at her; from her mother—where it had always been—and now, too, from her stepfather, Steve, and from her new little sister Mei-mei, already a precocious 16-month-old.

Mei-mei was born in China in the Year of the Goat. She had raven hair, rosy cheeks—and a soaring spirit. The exact date of Mei-mei's birth was not known—she had been found in a box placed in front of a police station in a town in northern China. But Naomi believed her little sister was born on the night of the big typhoon, the night Chen died—and that a part of his spirit was in them both.

"You have a brother in Canada, Mei-mei," Naomi whispered. "We both do." *And we'll meet him and be family, someday—you'll see—because this is our destiny. I'll make it so.*

My sincerest thanks go to Donna Mah, Jenny McKirdy, and Katie Meech for their advice and insight; to my critical pals Robin Minietta and Jeffrey Mead for their encouragement, friendship, and inspiration; to my friend and Regional Advisor for the Society of Children's Book Writers and Illustrators, Susan Sprengeler (who gets the last word); to my special circle of friends Sarah Wong Sin Ying, Sharon Wong Sin Lam, and Jovita Ho Kar Ching; and to D.P. and Emelyn Marquez, for their much-needed support.

_a b o u t   t h e   a u t h o r_

Karmel Schreyer lives in Hong Kong with her husband and two children. She works as a writer and editor of educational materials for Asian children. She is the daughter of former Governor General Ed Schreyer. She has worked in Paris, Florence, Tokyo, Jogjakarta, and Hong Kong.